BLACK LIGHT: OBSESSED

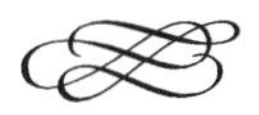

DANI RENÉ

e-Book ISBN: **978-1-947559-03-5**

Print ISBN: **978-1-947559-02-8**

Cover Art by Eris Adderly

obsession

əb'sɛʃ(ə)n/

noun

noun: **obsession**

the state of being obsessed with someone or something.

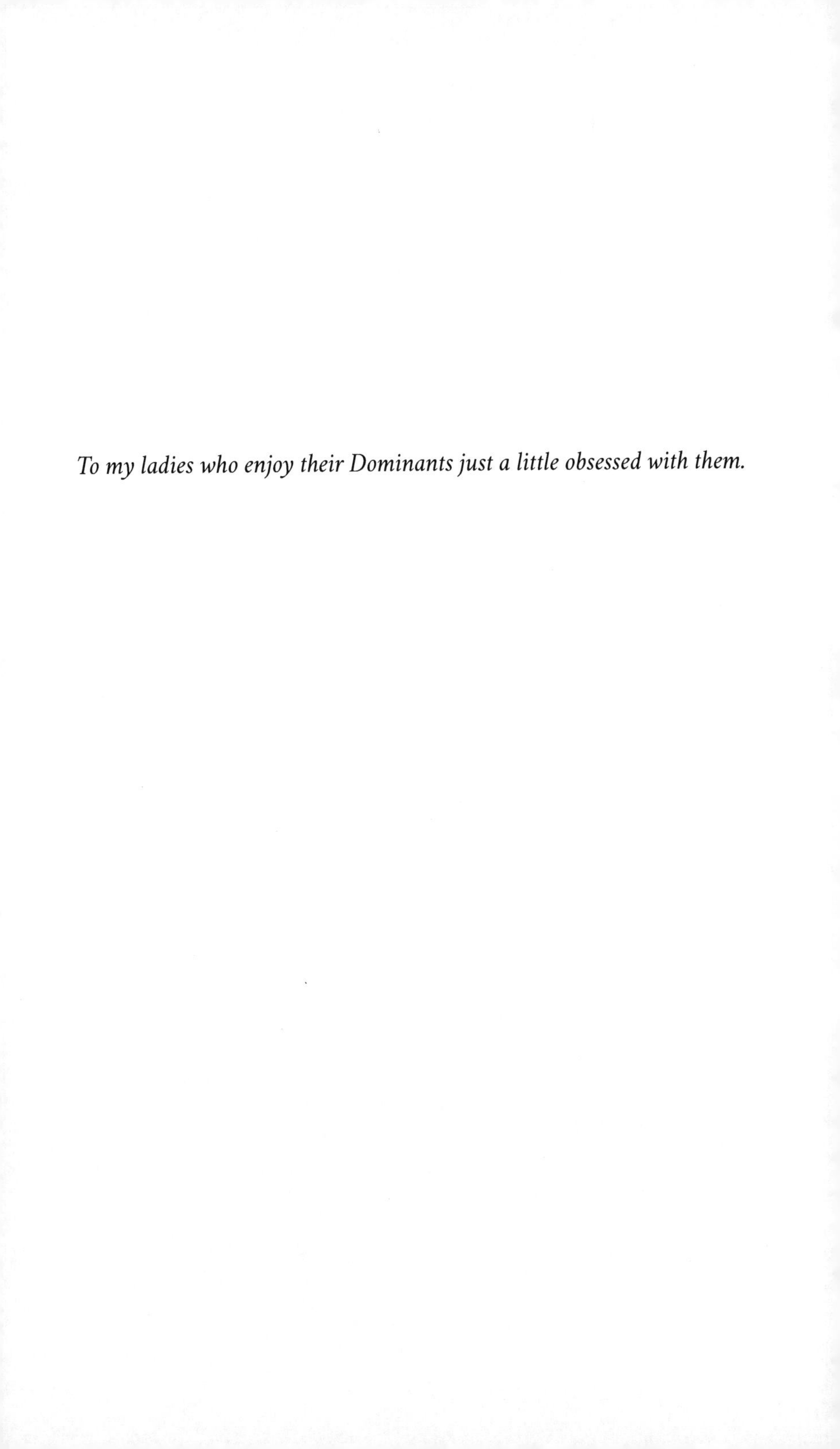

To my ladies who enjoy their Dominants just a little obsessed with them.

ACKNOWLEDGMENTS

I have to thank both Jennifer Bene and Livia Grant for the amazing opportunity to be writing in the Black Light series. I'm so honored, and humbled to have been chosen to join the family of this amazing world. You ladies are just incredible and it's been a wonderful privilege to work with Black Collar Press.

To my BETA ladies—Sheena, Alicia, Allyson, and Cat—thank you for loving Kian and Rosie and for taking the time out to read through the rough drafts and help me get them ready for the world.

My editor, Candy, you're always there at a moment's notice to polish up my words and make them shine. Thank you for everything!

To the readers, bloggers, and my fellow authors for sharing, reading, reviewing, and just being amazing, thank you a million times over!

PROLOGUE

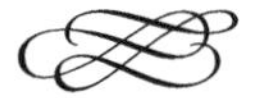

Roisin

THERE'S A SOFT GLOW FROM THE STREETLAMP, WHICH BATHES THE room in silvery light.

The house is silent, filled with heavy breathing and the stale stench of alcohol and sex. Dirty, vile, and putrid. I'm never sure of who I'd find on the other side of the door, so I stay locked in my bedroom when they have parties.

The two people who are now passed out without a care in the world will soon be left to their own devices. Shoving my clothes into the suitcase, I glance around, taking in the home I've spent the last two years in. But there's nothing more for me here. I waited until I was of legal age before I even thought about running. Any younger and I'd be worse off out there than I ever am in here.

Tomorrow I'll be eighteen and they won't want me here anymore. They'll soon be looking for a younger, more profitable baby.

Nobody wants me.

My parents made it clear when I was born, leaving me on the steps of a church. Talk about a poster child for a clichéd life story. Taken in by the pastor and his wife, I grew up Christian, praying and taught to believe in a God that has never been there for me.

Even though they gave me a roof to live under, it was never a home. Each Sunday, I was taken to church to pray for my sins, and every week, I'd just go out and do them again.

When I turned sixteen, they sent me away. Father Paulson's wife thought I was a devil child, so they put me in the system. No couple wants to adopt a sixteen-year-old, they want a cute baby they can coddle and coo with.

That's when Brady and Dana walked in and saw me. A meal ticket. They weren't parents. Far from it. They didn't give a shit if I was out doing drugs or if I was in my bedroom with one of the boys from school. No, I was only here because the State gave them money to keep me.

All the funds that were meant to go toward my schooling, clothes, and stationery were spent on more alcohol for their friends who visited every weekend. The men who would smirk at me like I was their next meal. I figured I was safe. But that's the first mistake I made.

Sighing, I glance in the mirror as I pull my long red waves into a messy bun. My blue eyes have lost their sparkle. All my life I've spent hiding because of my looks. Floppy jumpers, jeans, and trainers. A tom boy.

Everyone told me I'm pretty. A stunner. I didn't want that. I never did because underneath it all, it's my looks that got me in trouble. It's those big cerulean eyes, the pouty rose-colored lips, and the fair porcelain skin that ensured my life would turn to hell.

Most people would assume it's my adoptive father who did it.

Others would gossip that it was the priest and perhaps that's why I got sent away.

They may have had a part to play in my broken past, but there was so much more to it than that. Until I reached sixteen, I lived in a home that was focused on religion. The man who was a Father to many, took everything from me.

When I went to my second foster home, I knew as soon as I walked into the house, it would not be any better.

School was difficult for me. I didn't have friends. I didn't want any. But it was then when I'd given up hope, that I thought I'd found someone who saw me for who I am. The only boy I had ever trusted. Chad Hollister.

He noticed me. He asked me out.

For six wonderful months, I was happy. He doted on me. Made sure I was smiling from ear to ear every day. I believed he really liked the broken girl he learned I was. I thought that deep down, he wanted to love me.

But life doesn't afford girls like me a chance at love.

I'm broken into so many small pieces of myself that I know I can never be whole again.

When Chad saw me like that, he told me it's okay. He still wanted me. Once again, I trusted someone and got burned in the process. When we walked into prom two nights ago, he had sent photos of me naked on his bed to everyone in our school.

It turns out his group of friends made a bet that no guy could last a month with me and my fucked-up family. He told me in front of everyone how he'd been the one to draw the short straw and when one month turned into two, the six guys he hung out with promised to pay for his whole summer vacation down in Florida after graduation. They laughed at his confession, jeering him on.

They all saw me for who I really was.

And that's part of the reason I need to leave.

Eighteen and a runaway.

I'm not sure where I'm headed, but it will be better than here. As soon as I step out of my bedroom, the smell hits my nostrils, causing my stomach to roll. Vomit, sweat, and alcohol, mixed with the old cigarette smell that always hangs around the house, hits me square in the face.

I pull out my own packet of smokes, tapping a stick out and pressing it between my lips. The silver glint of my adoptive dad's Zippo calls to me. With a smirk, I snatch it up on my way to the exit. To my freedom.

As soon as the front door hits my ass on the way out, I light up my smoke, shoving the expensive item into the back pocket of my jeans, then head toward the bus stop. Since it's after midnight, I'm not expecting any public transport, but I'll wait.

The night is warm, balmy, heavy with the scent of the town I've spent the past two years in. Only a few hours outside of L.A. along the coast, I've always longed to escape to the big city. It's going to be a long ride to the place I've wanted to visit all my life. They call it the City of Angels, but it's so far from the truth. I've read stories about what happens there. I've lost myself in articles, stories from pop stars to actors who've lost everything in Los Angeles. Instead of angels, it's filled with devils and broken hearts. Dreams smashed on the sidewalk for all to see.

I won't miss the small town life, even if I have no idea what I'm running toward. My old life will soon be a distant memory.

Upon reaching the one main road in this shithole town, lights flicker from an oncoming car, the only vehicle out at this time of the night and I wonder just who is approaching me. When it nears, I notice it's a sleek silver Mercedes Benz. One of those fancy ones I know I'll never own.

Strolling further up the hill toward the center of town where I know there'll be early morning busses heading into L.A., I watch as he slows down, probably thinking I'm some fucking whore. He stops, rolls down his window, and leans over to drag his gaze over me. He looks like he's in his late twenties. Dark hair, big eyes that look blue or silver, I can't tell.

"Where you headed this late, darling?" His mouth tilts into a smirk, ravenous and hungry. That's what they all want when they look at me.

A fuck.

"Anywhere away from here."

He looks me up and down once more, nods, and unlocks his car. "Get in. I'll drive you down to the station where you can get a bus. I'm not leaving this hick town for a while yet, so you'll have to find your own way."

I stare at him for a moment, unsure of trusting a stranger. The last time I did that, it didn't go so well. But, it is the middle of the night and I have no place to go. Dropping my smoke on the concrete below my foot, I stomp it out, twisting my Chucks to kill it, and head toward the car.

"You're no serial killer or anything. Are you?"

He chuckles at my question, shaking his head as he regards me with a small smile. "There's no way I am, darling. Get in, I have to get home to my wife," he tells me, lifting his left hand to show me the thick gold band around his ring finger.

Knowing he's married doesn't change the fact this asshole could do things to me other men have already done. But, somehow, for some inexplicable reason, I get in the car. It's cool inside with the air conditioning blowing wildly from the vents. The leather seat below my ass squeaks as my jeans press against the smooth material.

"What's a guy like you doing in a hick town like this?" I question, using his words for the shithole I spent two years in.

"Used to live out here," he says, not looking at me. "Got out as soon as I could."

I stare at him for a moment, taking in his rugged jaw each time the light from the street lamp illuminates the inside of his car.

"What's your name, darling?" he questions, turning the steering wheel as we head down the long winding street.

I don't know why, but I lie. There were many times in my

childhood I was whipped for lying, but there's no longer anyone who can hurt me for doing as I please.

"My name's Rosie," I tell him, keeping my attention on the road. I know where I am, where we're going, so if he makes a wrong turn, I'll know. But he keeps his word, taking the road toward the bus station.

"You need to be careful, Rosie. Getting in a stranger's car could get you hurt," he warns, causing my eyes to veer his way. There's a genuine seriousness in his tone. Something I haven't heard in a long while.

"I know. But if I've already been killed inside, what difference does it make?"

My words are ominous, and he doesn't respond. Perhaps he doesn't know how, or he may never have expected me to say something like that. The rest of the drive is in utter silence.

I think about my meagre belongings as I take in his fancy car and I wonder if his kids are spoiled, or even if he has a family. The small laptop in my backpack that I managed to buy off Craigslist and the old mobile phone I got when I was living at the church are the only valuables I have.

"Here we are," stranger announces.

"Thanks," I tell him, meaning it. For the first time in my life I feel grateful for someone who did something for me without wanting something in return. Pushing the car door open, I step out.

"Hey," my savior calls to me, causing me to lean into his car once more. "Look after yourself, Rosie," he tells me.

"I'll try."

ROISIN - FIVE YEARS LATER

Fingertips brush along my curves.
Caress my slick flesh.
Taunt me.
Play me.
Fuck. Do it.
Hurt me so I can feel again.

Tapping the keys, I read the quote and reread it to make sure there aren't any spelling errors. Too many people don't notice it, but I do. The frustration of it crawls over my flesh, annoyed that they don't see their mistakes. My mind is blank once more. It hurts to move, to think.

Tapping the send key, I watch the slim blue upload bar above the post. The image I chose is perfect. Two slender fingers pressing down on a voluptuous hip. The skin is glistening with water droplets that shimmer under the light.

Bare.

Naked.

The new post is fresh on my feed. It only takes a minute before there are likes. Hearts. Bright red and happy. The color of blood. I don't know why I do this, put myself out there only to have anxiety twisting in my gut. The low swirl of a brewing storm knots and grips me. The claws of my familiar and dreaded fucked up mind.

My eyes are glued to the number of likes, and as the comments roll in, I smile. They devour the darkness like I knew they would. This is what I've become addicted to. Needing to see their approval.

So hot.
Filthy and sexy.
I'd fuck you.
Delicious tease.

Another smile.

Since I was younger I knew I wanted to write. To create worlds with words. To offer part of myself to people without them even knowing it. It was exciting to see people read something I'd written for the school paper and enjoy it.

Now, I work for a magazine where the real life tales I create are read by millions, and I hope deep down that my writing can help them too. The posts I make on my Instagram, however, are darker, more elicit, something that allows me to express my passion for the lifestyle I've always been intrigued by.

Pushing up from the bed, I pad over to the kitchen. The small space is tiled with white Italian ceramic squares that make up the back bar of the sink and kitchen counter. Silver taps twinkle in the dim light as I open one to fill the kettle.

Everything in my home is expensive, stylish, and luxurious.

It took me five long years to get where I am today, and as soon as I could afford my condo, I bought it out right. The man who sold it to me looked at me like I was a trust fund baby. If only he knew.

When I left home at eighteen, with nothing but a few hundred bucks and small rucksack, I vowed to be better than the past I left behind. And for the most part, I am. But there are times that all comes rushing back.

And I'm once again the little girl who had nobody to fight for her.

The teenager who was accused of being a slut.

And the eighteen-year-old runaway who would do anything to stay off the streets.

I watch the steam filtering from the spout of the stainless-steel electric kettle. My focus is so intense, it blurs everything beyond it.

I have a deadline to meet, but my mind is awash with thoughts on how to better my words. My website. My social media. For a recluse like myself, it's the only way I can have friends and not have a panic attack.

That is, besides my one good friend I've made along my rocky path here.

Greer McCleary.

We've known each other for a year. I call her my best friend, but that's a lie because she's my only friend. She's the complete opposite to me. A party girl who prefers the company of others to her own. Me, on the other hand, I love the solace of being alone.

A light vibration from my desk tells me there's someone looking for me. Perhaps someone I don't want to talk to, like my agent. When I signed a deal to publish my words, I did it online. There were no meetings. Nothing that would get me to leave my home.

Being based in Wilshire, I've become accustomed to ordering

all my groceries online to avoid going out, fighting the traffic, but also, my anxiety can be rather paralyzing. Most days, my contact with strangers is limited to the delivery guy at my door. Or Greer, who forces her way into my home. I don't mind so much, she's sweet, trying to get me to come out of my shell. There are however times I am forced to go into the office, or if Greer decides I need to go to the bar and have a drink with her. It's those times I need to psyche myself up and attempt being *normal* for an hour until I excuse myself and race home.

My whole life was spent hiding.

Bullied for my looks, my poor home life, and everything else they could pin on me, I figured out that the only person I can trust is myself. And I've not let anyone in since.

How a short, five-letter word can hurt so much is beyond me.

Once it's broken, there's no repairing it. There were too many people during my younger years who taught me to only think of myself. To watch my back when it comes to strangers, and more so, to never trust a friend.

Now I spend all my time online.

A social media addict, because even though I'd love to allow people into my life, my home, and my heart, fear has held me down. Pinned me in its vicious grip, causing me to flail in darkness when my nightmares appear.

The vibration starts again.

Sighing, I pick up my cell phone to find Greer's name on the screen, flashing at me, screaming at me to answer. Tapping the green circle, I put it to my ear.

"And to what do I owe this pleasure?" I tease, smiling despite my melancholy morning.

"Let's have lunch in the park," she says. It's not a question. She's always forcing me to go outdoors, to get fresh air.

"Why would we do that? Do you know how many bugs are on the grass? They can crawl—"

"God, you're such a bitch," she retorts playfully. That's one thing I know about my best friend. She's a girly girl. Any type of bug will have her running away screaming.

"I know, but that's why you put up with me."

Her sigh is the only sign that she's frustrated with me. I'm frustrated with myself. For so long I had convinced myself I was normal. But I know I'm not. I can't be. My gaze falls to my bare legs. The shorts I'm wearing reveal the only evidence that I'm far from normal.

"I do love you, and I do put up with you because I know this isn't forever. You can do this, you know?" She sounds so confident. I wish I could find her confidence.

"You're only saying that because you want to head out to Runway. That place is like a pit of celebrities and people who earn more in a day than you can even fathom."

"Listen, if I want to rub shoulders with the elite, I don't see anything wrong with that. What if we walked in and some hot, famous guy sweeps you off your feet?" This time, she giggles like a teenager.

"Oh really? Who would that be?" I play her game, but I can't help smiling at her infectious attitude. She knows it's difficult for me to put myself out there. It's downright frightening. My mind whirls with anxiety, my chest tightens, and every nerve in my body goes cold when I'm in a crowded place with nobody I know.

"You never know."

She's right. I need to get out. Do things.

"Fine, we'll see at the end of the week."

"That's what you said last time," she complains. "I'll talk soon, Dragon lady is coming."

Her voice drops to a hiss, and I know our senior editor and boss is heading her way. The line clicks, dying on me before I can say goodbye. Shaking my head, I giggle at Greer.

THE AIR IS CLEAN AND EVEN THOUGH WE'RE HEADING INTO SPRING, the weather is warmer than I anticipated when I woke up this morning. I pulled on a black woolen skirt with knee-high striped socks. Even though I'm twenty-three, I dress like I did when I was sixteen.

Some people say I haven't grown up. Perhaps I haven't, but somehow, it's the only way I can find comfort with who I am. Placing the lit cigarette between my lips, I pull deeply on the smoke. My lungs fill with the nicotine my body craves and I revel in the minty flavor.

I've smoked since I was fourteen. Stealing from the Pastor's secret stash he kept in his home office. His wife didn't know, at least, she didn't let on that she knew her husband had secret addictions. And smoking wasn't the only one.

I'd sneak in while he was away, and grab one or two cigarettes, hiding them in my bedroom. When they were asleep I'd sit out on the windowsill at night and watch the stars twinkle above me with promise. All I ever wanted was to be loved. To feel as if I was wanted.

The Hollywood sign shimmers in the early morning sunlight as I head to work. Normally, my office is my second bedroom within the security of my condo, but today, I have to meet with the editor of Plush Magazine and listen to her moan about some shit I don't really care about. She didn't want to talk to me on Skype about whatever assignment she has for me, so I'm forced to step outside my comfort zone. Thankfully, I live close to the office, which allows me to avoid the traffic which would only set my anxiety skyrocketing.

Three black Chevrolet Suburbans fly by and I wonder who's in them. Whenever I see those blacked out windows, my interest is piqued and I want to follow behind just to get a glance of the men in black.

A giggle escapes my lips when I recall the movie instead of the Secret Service. Sighing, I turn down a small side street to enter through the alleyway instead of the main entrance of the office building.

Being close to people sets me on edge, so I'd rather miss the crowds and head up the fire escape. When I reach the fourth floor, out of breath, I find Greer sitting at her desk.

"Rosie." She smiles as I near her. "I hear the dragon is out for flesh today," she utters under her breath in warning. Our senior editor, Gladys Caldwell, is one of the most difficult women when she's in a mood.

"Great," I mutter with resignation that I'm in shit.

I'm about to say something more when I smell her fake Dior perfume wafting from the hallway and I know my time is up.

"Rosie!" My name is squealed in her loud and boisterous New York accent. Even though we're on the West Coast, she brings with her a feel of the East and it makes me tense. My ex foster mom had that shrill screech when she called me. Only, she never called me by my name.

"Ms. Caldwell." I plaster on a fake smile and turn to her.

"I need you. There's an interview I'd love for you to work on." She gasps and pulls me along behind her toward her ornate office. The room is decked in rich purples, reds, and black. There's even a damn gold-legged glass desk, which to me is way beyond over-the-top.

"I don't do interviews," I tell her earnestly. She knew this when she hired me. My anxiety skyrockets when I'm put under pressure and that was the reason I told her I'd work from home. No people, no meetings, and none of this excitement that she seems to emanate.

"This"—she spins on her heel, almost knocking me to the ground—"is one you will want." With a flourish, she rounds her desk, reaching for a bright purple folder that has the Plush company logo on it. She hands it to me.

Sighing, I open it, but the photos inside knock the breath from my lungs. Gently, I lift one that catches my attention. A black and white curve of a woman's body is captured in dim light with her long blond hair hanging low on her back, almost to her ass.

The next one is another model, beautifully decked in satin and lace. The photographer has her long flowing hair knotted on top of her head. Her legs are splayed wide, her back to the lens, and her arms are intricately bound in a deep crimson rope.

"What are these?" I glance up at my boss, who's smiling like the Cheshire cat. She's pleased it's caught my attention.

"I don't know his real name, but he signs all his photos with a Master K. People wonder if it's perhaps someone famous trying to keep his real identity under wraps, but there's no information on the website, or even on social media accounts." She sighs dramatically as if she's just lost the lottery. Slumping into her chair, she picks up her coffee mug and takes a long gulp before meeting my curious stare.

"So how am I meant to interview this person when we have no information about them?" I question, settling in the purple suede chair opposite her. My heart is thumping at the imagery I've just seen. My body prickles with awareness of who he is. A shadowed stranger. Someone who doesn't want to be known, but I want to meet him. I want him to capture me in that light. Bound and helpless.

"I have IT on the case. They're tracking down the information I asked. Name, email, whatever they can find on our anonymous photographer."

My eyes drop to the photos again, my finger trailing the curve of a breast, wondering if he touched the model in the photo. Was she his girlfriend? Perhaps even a mistress? *Master K.* Even his name sends a shiver down my spine.

"Fine. When you have contact details send them to me. I'll get it done." I rise, meeting her inquisitive stare. "Is that all?"

"Yes, and get that review about that romance novel you're meant to be reading to me by tonight. I need it for our next edition."

"Sure." I smile, holding on to the folder with the photos for a moment longer before reaching to place it on her desk.

"No, you keep them. Use it as inspiration."

Nodding, I smile and exit her office without any more words. I can't find my voice, because all I can think about is the man behind the lens.

"And? Are you fired?" Greer giggles when she glances up.

"You know she won't fire me. Who'll read those smutty books she keeps signing up for?" I quip playfully. My best friend nods.

"Tonight? Drinks?" she questions, knowing I'll refuse. I'm not fond of going out, but there are times she'll persuade me to head out for a glass of wine.

"Not tonight, I have a review to write," I tell her. "Maybe Friday?" It's two days away. That will give me time to research Master K.

"Don't bail on me, bitch," she taunts.

"Shut it." My retort is just as playful as our friendly banter normally is. Being honest and open with someone is new to me, but something about the feisty raven-haired woman is enough to have me opening up about my life. She has a way with words. A personality you can't help but love.

The elevator takes me back down to the entrance foyer. As soon as I step out of the building, I inhale the air that's filled with the scent of coffee from the shop next door. I follow the smell and step inside the air-conditioned store. There's a short queue, which I join. The tables are all full, so when I finally place my order, it's for a to-go cup.

Being out of my condo for a little while feels good, but I know it won't last long. Perhaps I'll sit in the park and look through the photos again. When I think of the salacious shots, a trickle of desire races over me. The need to know who this man is still sits at the forefront of my mind, which is an overpowering feeling, one that as much as I try, I can't ignore.

KIAN

Buttoning my suit jacket, I head into the headquarters of my agency that allows us to keep celebrities out of the media. We also assist those who are able to afford our premium price with private investigation services. It's been almost ten years since I first opened the doors, filling me with pride and self-assurance that I have something I worked my ass off to kickstart from the ground up. Running the agency allows me to work my own hours, giving me time off when I need it.

The best part is that it allows me to use my photography skills.

I was born and bred in Scotland, but I moved to the US because my wife wanted to build a life close to her parents. Once we'd settled, I found a love of investigative work. Even though it was my dream to work with the Central Intelligence Agency in Washington, I knew I couldn't live in the same place where I lost my wife. The love of my life. The woman who still for the most part owns my heart. I still wonder what would've happened had I not spent twenty-four-seven in the field instead of at home with my now ex-wife and daughter.

Even though I worked my ass off to get where I am today, living the dream, I regret not giving Siobhan the support she needed when the time came to step up and be a husband and father. Now, all I have is my work.

"Ryland."

I turn at the sound of my last name, finding one of my best friends smirking over at me. He's in his early-forties, only a few years older than me, and he's already been giving me shit about hitting the big four-o.

"There's a new client meeting us at ten. I'm heading up to the conference room to set up," he informs me.

It's just hit nine, so I have time to grab a coffee before I have to listen to the shit going on that we'll have to once again step in and fix.

"Who is it? Some famous asshole who got caught fucking a teeny bopper?" I question as I follow him into the canteen.

The room itself is full of agents dressed in black suits and crisp white shirts. Standard uniform. Some have earpieces, others are glued to their phones.

"Ha, you wish. Nothing's that fucking easy, man. It's some dude wanting us to investigate his stepdaughter's whereabouts. Apparently she ran away from home, only eighteen, and he's worried," Gibson says with a grim expression on his face. I know why. Many teens run away from home due to abuse or some shit, and if he's looking for her, it can't be good.

Don't get me wrong, I don't know this guy at all, but stepfathers, or even blood-related dads looking for runaway daughters tend to lead us down one sordid path. One I hate to travel down even on my darkest days.

"I don't trust assholes like that," I tell him. I would refuse the job, but I want to hear about it first. Then I'll make my decision.

"Neither do I, to be honest, but let's hear him out," Gibson tells me, as if reading my mind. That's why we get along so well. He trusts as little as I do. "However, I do have a proposition for you," he utters, gulping his coffee.

"Oh yeah?" I quip as I pour my coffee into the mug that has my name inked on it. When I turn to my partner, he's smiling like a fucking cat that's got the cream. "What?"

"Tonight, Black Light. Me and you, head out there and enjoy the evening with a pretty girl on our arm."

It sounds intriguing. I've been with him a few times, even signed up as a member when I finally realized it was the only thing keeping me sane.

"Mmmm," I murmur, taking a sip of the scorching hot liquid I'm hoping will get me through the meeting. "Sounds tempting, but I think I might stay in tonight."

He chuckles, shoving his hands in the pockets of his slacks. "Listen to me, you stay in far too much. I know Siobhan left, but you can't let that deter you. There's a world of beautiful women out there waiting for you."

"Jesus, Gibson." I chuckle, glancing at him. He's dead fucking serious as well. "Let me think about it. There's shitloads to do today and I don't know what time I'll get out of this place."

"Fine, but there's an event happening in a couple of weeks, masquerade ball with all the beauties out for a Dominant to show them the ropes. Don't miss that," he warns.

"Yeah, yeah," I respond, heading out to the conference room.

It's deserted when we arrive, and I know soon there'll be papers strewn all over the table, with my laptop firing at a million miles a second.

Most of my day is spent indoors, researching and attempting to find lost loved ones, or digitally following spouses as they head off to have affairs across the city. And other times, I'm in here using new ways of cleaning up profiles of celebrities with threats, lawsuits, and a few other colorful ways of getting offending videos and images of them off the Internet.

"So, did that asshole who came in here the other day ever find out about his wife banging the pool boy?" Gibson questions as he sets up his laptop, attaching it to the projector screen.

"Yeah, apparently he was livid because the boy was Cuban, didn't give a shit about him being eighteen," I inform him.

I've had some strange clients through my door over the years. Seen it all, as they say. I've understood the underlying rage that fuels people of different cultures. Sure, English and Scottish aren't too vastly different, but there's anger that brews beneath the surface.

"Since you've been married, do you ever think you'll do that again? Commit to one woman?" Gibson asks with a chuckle, which has me laughing.

"Never again. It was shitty the first time and I doubt it will ever be any better. I'm a workaholic. A woman needs a partner who'll put her first," I tell him, settling into the seat.

"But you'd collar a submissive?"

I think about it for a moment, then nod. "Perhaps. If I found one worthy enough," I answer him honestly. "It's not something I'm outwardly looking for, you know that."

"And you think you could find one in the City of Angels?" he asks, opening the door for our receptionist. I don't get a chance to respond, because she informs him our client is here. Although his words have my mind wandering. Los Angeles. The City of Angels, as it's so famously called, however, I know there's no purity left in this shithole.

I'm not angry.

I'm not jealous.

But when Siobhan told me this place held nothing for her, I watched her walk out with our daughter. I see her every third week in an attempt to make sure she knows who I am. I've never been scared in my life, but with her, I'm fearful she'll grow up resenting me for how things were left with her mother. I don't want to fuck up my daughter's life like I did my ex-wife's.

I vowed I'd never let Siobhan steal her from me. I watch my baby girl. I always will. She may not know I'm there, but I am there for my daughter. Even when her mother doesn't know I am.

Having limited time with her, I find myself obsessing over what she's doing, what her likes and dislikes are. It hurts saying goodbye when I take her back to her mother, but my ex-wife is adamant with her demands of my time with my daughter.

One day, I'll walk into Cassidy's life and get to hold her in my arms and never let go. One day.

Two days after they left the home I'd bought for us, I walked into Black Light for the first time. I became obsessed with the women. They offered me everything, submitting to me as if I were their savior. But I'm nothing of the sort. No. I'm the devil incarnate. A man who couldn't even keep his wife because of his predilections.

When I have a case, I become intoxicated by it. My life revolves around the mark, the person I'm following, helping, trying to find. The door opens as a man dressed in an expensive tailored suit stalks into the room.

"PI Ryland." He smirks, closing the distance between us. "It's good to meet you." Offering his hand, he stops before me and I decide I don't like the asshole. I've always been good at reading people, and he's no different.

"And you are?" I question, shaking his hand.

"I'm Mr. Prescott," he says as he pulls one of the chairs out and settles in it. Once he's comfortable, he glances between me and Gibson.

"What can we do for you?" my partner questions, seating himself beside me.

"My stepdaughter has disappeared with her boyfriend. She's just turned eighteen. I'm concerned." He shoves a small black USB drive across the table and I slot it into the laptop. I pull up the folder with photos.

There are some flirty images of a beautiful blonde girl with big blue eyes. Her smile is bright and I can see how she's possibly garnered stepdaddy's attention.

I turn to him. "And she's been gone for a month?"

"Yes," he starts. "She's always been a good girl. I mean… she's never done drugs, or went out partying with friends. I don't know what to make of it. Then she found this boy, well… a man I should say—"

"Man?" I question.

He nods. "Yes, he was in his mid-thirties and I told her he's far too old for her, but being a single dad isn't easy. Especially when she knows I'm not her real father."

"And what makes you think she's still in L.A.?"

"Open the video." He gestures with his chin toward the laptop and I click on the file. As soon as it plays on screen, my heart kicks wildly in my chest.

I don't say anything. Instead, I watch in awe as this young girl is inhaling line after line of white powder from the table in the middle of a wild party. Kids who can't be older than eighteen laugh, falling beside her on a purple sofa.

The club is dimly lit, but I recognize the furnishings.

She's in Velvet.

It's one of the newer clubs that's just opened. Well-known in the celebrity circles for the shit that goes down in there. I've been inside a few times, pulling out girls who are drugged out of their minds.

"We'll find her," I tell him.

The fear that grips me at the thought of her being my daughter sets me in motion. I'm on my feet and shaking his hand. As much as I don't like or trust the asshole, I know this girl is in trouble and I'm going to make it my mission to find her.

"My bank will transfer the cash to you now," he informs me, tapping something on his phone. I realize he's on a banking app. The early cash flow will come in handy to get my guys out there scouring the clubs and dealers.

"I'll call you in a day or two once we have information. Give us at least forty-eight hours to get a handle on her and this guy she's with."

He stops me as I stalk by him, and I turn to look at him. His mouth is pursed in a grim line. "Find her, because when you do, I'll make sure she doesn't run again."

His words are menacing, and I know Gibson's noticed it as well because he clears his throat in an attempt to distract me. He knows me far too well. I wouldn't think twice about putting this asshole six-feet under.

"If you touch my fucking suit again, I'll break your hand. I know how to do my job. Do not fuck with me," I hiss in his face. Leaning in, I make sure he can't look away. "And let me make one thing clear. I said I'll find your daughter, but I didn't say I'll return her to you."

"I fucking paid you!"

"Get out of my office. When I find her, you'll be informed. She will decide if she wants to go home, or to rehab, and somehow, I have a feeling she'd prefer to spend her days and nights around people going cold turkey rather than be in the same house as you."

His face turns a bright shade of red. One I normally enjoy seeing on a pretty little ass, but with him glaring at me, I can't help chuckling.

"I do my job, you pay my fee. I'll find her, but don't think for one fucking second that I trust you." My voice has a cool edge to it. The threat I just grit out in anger hangs between us, and he backs down.

"I just want my baby girl back," he says in a calmer tone than before. Perhaps I should believe him, but I don't.

I don't respond. Instead, I head out of the conference room and down the hall to my office. "Bianca, get me a coffee, please. This is going to be a long day," I call to our receptionist, who's sitting at her desk when I pass by.

"Yes, sir." She smiles brightly. Her blonde hair shimmers and I momentarily picture her bound to my bed. Shaking my head of the wayward thought, I step into my office and shut the door. I've never fucked anyone I worked with. It's bad business bringing relationships—physical or emotional—into a workplace.

Perhaps a visit to Black Light will be in my best interest.

Opening my laptop, I pull up my search engine software. There are a million different programs I can use, but this will get me results faster. I tap in her name and hit the search button. Bianca strolls in holding a large mug of steaming coffee.

"Thank you." I offer her a grin and notice the gentle pink on her cheeks.

"Let me know if you need anything else." She smiles before leaving and I wonder if that was an offer of something more.

No. I refuse to walk down that path.

Turning my attention to the video once more, I attempt to focus on clues in the screen. This asshole pissed me off today. I hate men like him. He's allowed his fortune to go straight to his shiny, bald head, thinking money can buy everything. Perhaps it can, but it certainly doesn't get you respect. The man is nothing more than an overgrown baby with a complex that sets my body alert with the need to punch him in that smug grin.

Opening my emails, I type out a request to keep a lookout for the pretty blonde teenager. Once that's done, I pull up my photography website. There are a few new message requests. One for an interview, which I politely decline. The other messages are all beautiful women wanting to be photographed.

I respond to them eagerly, wondering how delicious they'd look in black and white. I have two lined up for this weekend. I enjoy what I do. Photography has been a love of mine since I was in school. Even then, when I had a small disposable my father bought me, I reveled in capturing things, time, people, objects.

My passion will always lie there, but the persona I created needs to stay secret. I want it separated from this investigative life. Shutting down the browser with my messages, I focus back on the task at hand.

A long day indeed.

ROISIN

Your touch on my naked flesh is all I desire.
Mark me. Fuck me.
I'm your pet.
Harder. Faster. Deeper.
The delicious ache of sex.

THE SMALL BLUE BAR SLIDES ALONG THE SCREEN. IT'S ALMOST there.

Anticipation thrums in my veins. It's almost as if it's vibrating.

The need for recognition. For acceptance.

I watch as the numbers appear. More and more tapping the small heart. They love the post. Wanting to see what I'll come up with next. Opening my laptop, I open my browser, typing in the name on the card, Master K. As soon as I hit search, a website pops up in the first line of my search engine.

My heart races when I click on it. A black background, darkness follows this man. The first thing I do is click on the *about* section.

MASTER K IS A WELL-KNOWN PHOTOGRAPHER. TAKING A BREAK FROM his rather stressful day job, he enjoys spending time amongst the BDSM community where he is most himself. His images have been sold to galleries across the world. The only thing we don't know about Master K is what he looks like.

Damn.

My frustration niggles at me. I want to know who this man is. The one behind the lens. My curiosity is piqued. I click on the *Gallery*, which slowly loads onto hundreds, and I mean hundreds, of black and white images.

ALL OF THEM ARE PERFECTLY SHADOWED SO THERE AREN'T ANY parts of the woman showing that might make it seem pornographic. The curves of the woman seems like his muse was the same person.

She's beautiful. Even in the shadow of the images, I can tell there's an elegance to her, something gentle, yet shy.

It's a contrast to her sitting naked and being published on such a public forum. I head back to my phone, tapping in the Instagram name, and when his profile comes up, I hit follow. I scroll through the images on the screen and notice there hasn't been a new image on this particular one in almost two years.

Strange.

Perhaps they've broken up. My stomach flips at the thought of him being single. *Would I want to get involved with a man who so openly exposes women? And how many has he even been with?*

I head back to my laptop, to the screen where I'm greeted with the erotic images that make me want to meet him.

Opening the direct messaging on my Instagram, I stare at the white bar where I can type out my words. *Do I tell him I want to be his model?* I don't know how many moments pass before I drum up the courage.

Your photos are intriguing. I want to learn more. My words would be an amazing combination alongside your images.

I DOUBT HE'D RESPOND. PERHAPS HE HAS PEOPLE WHO DO THIS FOR him. Setting my phone down, I close the website. I have work to do, but even as I open up my manuscript, my mind is still plagued by the idea of posing for him.

Could he make me beautiful?

My phone dings with an alert just then, causing my heart to leap into my throat. The small notification tells me I've received a reply. *It's him.* I'm nervous when I pick up my cell, swiping the screen and finding a bright red dot against the app logo. It's there taunting me.

Inhaling a deep breath, I tap the square and it opens. The message pops up. In black and white is his response.

I know it's him because of what it says. What he says to me.

My photos are what keeps me sane. You speak of intriguing, but so are you pet. Would you have the courage to sit for me? To take off your armor you wear for the everyday world?

MY HEART LEAPS INTO MY THROAT. MY FINGERS ARE SHAKY AS I read, reread, and for a third time devour his words. I want to shout yes! To scream it. To tell him that all I want is to feel beautiful and allow the pain, the fear, and everything else that holds me back to no longer be there.

I want to be free. To let go of all the stress of life. But I don't tell him because I'm shy, scared that if I'm honest, he'll disappear. Instead, I tap out a fairly generic response.

This is new to me. Perhaps you can call me a virgin to taking my clothes off willingly. I don't know if I have the courage. But I'd like to try.

ONCE I HIT SEND, I DON'T WAIT LONG. IT'S AS IF HE'S BEEN SITTING there waiting for my response. The three dots dance along the bottom of the screen. He's replying. I can't help smiling. This feeling of fluttering wings in my stomach is ever present. Something I'd never really felt until high school and even then, it was a curse instead of a blessing.

His response pops up beneath mine.

Then you'll have to learn to obey. To do as I say. When I'm with a woman, she is to allow me to lead her. I will teach you how to feel confident. I will indeed take your stress away. But, you need to realize, pet, this life is not for everyone. There's a darkness that most never see, but if you allow yourself to submit to it, I promise you'll fly.

WORDS.

The only thing I've ever had are words. Whether they were lies, or even blanketed truths, it's what I've held onto for so long. Now, as I read his promise, I want more. And that in itself is scary. Because men have never really been honest with me. *So how do I trust a stranger I've never even seen?* My phone vibrates in my hand once more with his reply and I eagerly open it, my stomach fluttering at the words my eyes devour.

You know, most women run away when they see how much you can leave behind. Letting go scares them. It makes them worry about what will happen when they don't have control. But you see, control is what holds you back. Allow yourself to feel, pet.

I WANT TO FEEL. I WANT HIM TO TEACH ME. MY FINGERS MOVE ON their own, typing out a response I didn't expect.

I'll think about it. I'm not saying no, but I need a day to think.

I HIT SEND, BREATHING DEEPLY TO CALM MY NERVES, TO HOPEFULLY calm my racing heart. Once again, his message comes through immediately. I wonder where he is, what he's doing.

You can take as long as you need. When you're ready, reach out.

I WONDER ABOUT HOW MUCH HE CAN OFFER ME. WILL THIS BE something that can perhaps allow me to free my anxiety and finally just be normal? I've never really thought about being spanked or tied down. My experience is limited to what I've already endured at the hands of a man who I trusted most of my short life. Even though he didn't take me, he did do things that I know were wrong.

It was when I finally left that home and moved into a place that was party central for the couple who was meant to be my parents, I realized sex was used as a payment. I learned from the age of sixteen, watching my foster mother give men sexual favors for drugs, alcohol, whatever she needed. And her husband would watch. He'd get off on it.

I don't want to be like that. I vowed I'd be different. Perhaps if I allowed someone to show me, to give me pleasure I can't find myself.

Do I call you Master K? Or do you have a name?

I WATCH IN SUSPENSE AS HE CONTINUES TO TYPE OUT HIS RESPONSE. I imagine his fingers moving along the smooth screen. Are they rough and calloused? Will his touch instill a safety inside me I've never once felt?

Ha, you only call me Master once you've submitted to me, my pet. For now, you're to call me K.

SUBMISSION.

I've read about it. The romance books I have on my bookshelf all talk about it. I've even spent nights reading about it online. Intrigued by how women can kneel for a man. And how they can allow themselves to be bound, helpless to the pleasure and pain.

The thought of having someone who you trust enough to allow them to see you so vulnerable, so open and willing to do as they wish, must be a rather powerful emotion. Dominant or Master doles out the pain but also gives pleasure beyond the imagination. And I'm certain that is the only way to feel free.

And if I wanted to learn from you, but find another man to submit to?

I WATCH WITH BATED BREATH AS THOSE DOTS JUMP AROUND, LEAPING with his response being tapped out. I wonder what he does as a day job. Perhaps he's a mechanic, getting his hands dirty every day. Or maybe he's a fancy lawyer, an actor. My mind is racing a million miles a minute before his message appears.

If you only want to learn, I can teach you. But before we enter any agreement, you need to be honest with me. If you're not, this will never work. Am I understood?

HIS GRUFF TONE THAT FILTERS OFF THE MESSAGE CAUSES MY THIGHS to squeeze together. My nipples harden when I imagine him holding my shoulders, crashing me against the wall and pinning me between the hard surface and his body. Perhaps his one hand moves toward my neck, holding me in place. Once again, the thought makes me tingle, my skin prickling at the images that are now playing through my mind.

Understood.

-

Good girl.

Two simple words.

They hold a power I never knew existed. Because as I read

them, I smile. I nod to myself. Am I really a good girl? Or is doing this so wrong? Another message from him comes through.

How old are you?

-

I'm twenty-three.

THERE'S NO RESPONSE FOR A MOMENT AND I WONDER IF HE'S NOT expected that. Maybe he wants someone younger, or older. Maybe he's far too old for me. I'm pondering all the possibilities when he gives me the answer I needed. The response I craved.

Perfect. Young, beautiful, and eager to learn. You'll do well under my guidance, pet.

I SMILE. I SMILE MORE THAN I HAVE IN YEARS. MY HEART IS FILLED with anticipation and excitement. I want to race out of here and find him. I want to feel his commanding words whisper along my skin. I want to feel his fingers drift along the curves of my body.

I respond.

Thank you.

SETTING MY PHONE DOWN, I PICK UP MY MUG AND GULP DOWN THE last dregs of my coffee, already needing a refill and it's not even lunch time yet. My stomach growls with a reminder that I haven't eaten at all. The morning was spent searching for Master K and now that I've found him, I'm ready to start my day.

Padding to the kitchen, I open the fridge and grab two eggs, the bacon, and some cheese. My food choices are limited since I haven't ordered anything in a while, and I haven't been out of the condo in over a week.

I go about my kitchen preparing a small breakfast, along with another full mug of coffee. It doesn't take long and once I'm propped on my sofa, I dive into the meal without breathing. I'm ravenous. I swallow down the food and when I finally sit back, I feel the need to take a nap.

The vibration on my phone is incessant and I take my coffee back to my desk. The screen is lit up like a Christmas tree with notifications. One from Greer, and the others from *him.* I open his first.

I'll set tasks over the next few days. This will get you ready for what I have in mind.

-

Are you there?

-

We don't have to start until you're ready. Perhaps I was being overzealous. I'm sorry. Take your time and I'll be here when you find you're ready.

My fingers move quickly but shakily across the screen.

I'm here. Sorry, I made breakfast. I'm ready. Give me tasks and I'll work through them. I spend my days at home because my job allows me to work from here.

He responds instantaneously.

Perfect. I have a meeting now. I'll message you once I'm done.

My heart is still thudding in my chest from a conversation with him, knowing that I should bring up the interview. I should ask him the questions I need to, but I can't bring myself to do it. Work is the last thing I want to talk about when I see his messages. I glance at my laptop. The manuscript sitting before me is blank, waiting for more words, but the only ones I can find are *him.* I want to tell him everything. I want him to drink me in, like a fine wine, something to be savored. My eyes fall to my hands, lost in thought as I wonder if he'd really want someone like me. I fucked up so many things in life, I just want to do this one thing right.

INSPIRATION FOR THE ARTICLE HITS ME THEN. MY FINGERS FLY OVER the keyboard, tapping out an anonymous confession that I know Plush Magazine would run. They do self-help articles all the time. So, now that I've got the idea, words flow through me. From the beat of my heart all the way down to the tips of my fingers.

Once I hit my thousand word limit, I do a read through, editing as I go. Adding and deleting what isn't needed. Sitting back, I do one final read through and find that it's perfect to send to one of the editors on the team.

There's one thing Ms. Caldwell doesn't let us do—edit our own work. I open my email, attach the document, and send the email. Feeling accomplished, I turn my attention back to Instagram. I save one of Master K's images onto my phone, I pull up the app, and tap out something to go alongside it.

In the darkness of our desire
The lust that resides within us
You set me free
With hands of steel, and a mouth of fire,
You take me to that place I never want to return from

THE IMAGE SLOWLY POSTS ALONG WITH THE HASHTAGS AND QUOTE. A second later, there it is—the likes, comments, and reposts appear. I've tagged him in the photo, given credit where it's due. I don't know if he'll hate what I've done, but I'll find out soon enough.

Remembering the message from my best friend, I open it to find an image of her latest conquest, asking for my approval.

The girl is crazy. She hits up Tinder more times than I would care to count. She's indeed not a bookworm like I am. I'm about to respond when she calls.

"Hey," I answer, knowing I've taken too long to answer her message and that's why she's about to chew me out.

"I need to know what you think."

"He's okay. I mean, he's a bit too pretty boy for me," I tell her.

She sighs at my response. "Fine, I'll meet him tonight and see how pretty he really is." She giggles at that. Sometimes, I don't know how we're friends. I mean, is there even a rule to say that your friends have to like the same things you do? If not, she and I are like that. She's oil and I'm vinegar. Bad analogy, but it works.

"I can't wait to hear all about it," I tell her wryly, knowing she's going to give me every single detail of what happens.

"Oh, you will, sweetheart. Can we go for dinner tomorrow, maybe—"

"You know where I live," my tone is serious. I'm not a clubbing type of girl.

"Fine, I'll bring the pizza to you. I'll call you later for advice on my outfit."

She hangs up before I can respond. I always enjoy spending

time with Greer, but after the day I've had, my thoughts drift back to Master K. He said he'd contact me again, and I can't help but feel hopeful that he truly will. That he wasn't saying it to placate me. I wonder if I'll get to meet my mysterious photographer soon.

I hope I do.

KIAN

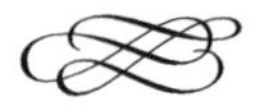

As soon as I pull into the drive I notice there's no sign of my neighbors who are normally out in their garden with friends, drinking and having a good time. It's almost eight and I know Gibson is probably waiting on me, but I need a shower before I head to Black Light.

I head into the house without a backward glance.

My house is large enough to hold a goddamn football stadium, but it's empty. Cold and barren. Like the person I've become. Yes, I photograph beautiful women who offer their bodies to me. Giving me everything; allowing me to spank, whip, bind them, but once the scene is through, they leave. I see them at their most vulnerable, but deep down, there's no affection.

Shrugging off my suit jacket, I hang it on the coat hook and make my way to my modern kitchen. The small cabinet near the patio door beckons and I pull it open to find the bourbon I've hidden from sight until tonight.

I'd spent far too long in a drunken stupor when Siobhan left me, and when I finally got myself back on track, my business running smoothly, the last thing I wanted or needed was this shit fucking it up. But tonight, I need it.

Pouring a double shot into a tumbler, I gulp it down in one swallow, savoring the burn down my throat. I refill the glass and trudge toward the steps that will take me up to the bedroom. My muscles are tense, aching with the frustration of the asshole clients we work with on a daily basis.

When I bought this house after Siobhan left me, I ensured that everything in it, from the furniture, to the colors on the walls, was mine, my choice, my taste. The black and white furniture, along with the dark wood antique cabinets, are a contrast in both color and style. Old world and modern. An en suite bathroom attached to the bedroom has also been turned into a space with clean lines. No flowery shit.

I strip off and step into the two-person shower. Turning on the taps, I allow the cold water to slap me awake and a hiss escapes my mouth. The water is like pinpricks of agony to my body, but I revel in it. I need it to forget the fucking day I had.

I haven't checked my phone, but that doesn't mean the girl who's been messaging me hasn't lingered in my mind.

All day, she's been in the back of my thoughts. The sweet innocence of her is intoxicating. It's been a long while since I took someone who's not been in this life before.

Tying a towel around my waist, I head into the bedroom and pick up my phone. Notifications have blown up over the past few hours. When I open the app, I find a tag from her, one of my photos with her elicit words.

I read the caption, once, twice. By the third time I'm enamored. I tap the heart, then hit comment.

Words so illicit should be celebrated, sweet.

I CAN'T BELIEVE THIS GIRL HAD SUCH FILTHY THOUGHTS IN HER mind. But it's like they say, it's always the innocent ones.

Setting the phone on the bed, I make quick work of getting dressed. My black slacks and a crisp white shirt ensure I'm dressed the part. This is who I am down to my core.

Master K.

My phone vibrates and I eagerly grab it. A response from her sends a tingle of awareness through me.

Only, it's not her, it's my partner telling me he's on his way. I don't respond because I'll be leaving in a few moments.

Opening the app, I check her profile, making sure I have notifications turned on. For the most part I'll be able to check, but as soon as I enter the club I won't have my phone till I leave.

I consider leaving another message for her but don't want to come across too eager. She did say she needs a day to think about it, but it's her words that have caught my attention.

I slip into the driver's seat of my Maserati, my body thrumming, the words she posted still replaying in my mind like a film reel on repeat.

I weave through the L.A. traffic. Even though it's late, there are still a number of cars heading home. It's the only thing I hate about this city, the fucking traffic.

My phone pings from the console and as much as I want to pick it up, I force myself to focus on the road. It might not be her. I don't want to get my hopes up and find it's not.

The lights of the city flit by as I make my way to the one place I know will offer me solace. The one place my mind can be set at ease, because I know for a fact I won't be able to do it at home.

The temptation to call her, to force her to talk to me, thrums through me. My muscles are tense with the memory of our messages.

I could have her kneeling for me. Submitting to my every

whim. The almost virgin-like way she spoke of this lifestyle makes my erection throb with need to violate that sweet innocence.

I pull up to the large coal-colored gates. They slide open, allowing me entrance to the mansion that beckons with all the dark delights that await me.

Runway West.

The club has been like a home to me. On the surface, it's a beautiful, well-known nightclub, but it's when you delve deeper into the mansion that you find its carnal delights—Black Light. The club where I can be myself. I can let go of all the stress of my job and enjoy the scenes being played out. And every now and then, I find myself taking a submissive and devouring her body like she craves so much.

I don't have to say a thing to anyone on my way in. Even as I slip my phone into the locker, with one last look, I notice she hasn't replied. Perhaps I've scared her off. Too bad. I'll have to find another willing toy to play with tonight.

"Kian," the voice comes from behind me, one I recognize far too well.

When I turn to face her, I note she's looking different. Her beautiful skin is caked in makeup, those dark eyes that I loved watering with tears for me are bloodshot, and I know this life has gotten to her in the worst way.

Not everyone can handle the submissive side. Offering up your life, body, mind to someone isn't easy. This is why I'm so careful with the women I choose.

"Misty." I offer her a kind smile, but when she glances at me, I notice she's been crying.

The problem with being so in tune with the submissives I've come across is that I care. I want them to find the man who will offer them what they so desperately need.

Domination.

"I've thought about you." She smiles, looking at me like I'm her savior, but I'm far from that. Nowhere near being anyone's knight in shining armor. I can't even look after myself.

"I have to go, but you take care," I tell her, turning and leaving her in the foyer as I make my way into the club. It's crowded, people milling around, men with women under their arms, looking at them like they're the king of the world.

I used to have that.

Now, all I have are messages from a woman I've never seen.

"Kian." Gibson's voice comes from the bar. Mikael Gibson has been my sounding board when it came to this life, to learning and exploring my Dominant needs. Offering advice when I asked, he's also offered me a friendship I know wouldn't have come if we didn't have such similar interests. He's seen me at my roughest, and he's also seen me when I was happy. Even though that happiness was short-lived, it was real. No other woman has challenged me in so long.

Until…

Shaking my head of the errant thought, I settle in beside him, gesturing for a drink as the barman slides our way. The place is sleek, sexy, and elegant, and even the staff have an air of sophistication.

"I'm late," I tell him, hoping he won't question me further. But then again, I've known him most of my life. Of course he's going to wonder.

"Tell me who she is."

Sighing, I lift the glass, gulping the harsh liquid as I watch the bar staff move about. I can feel his eyes burning into me. The questions hang in the air as I drink my bourbon. Not my alcohol of choice, but it's there, so it will have to do.

"Come on, man," he huffs beside me.

"I don't know who she is," I tell him, turning to face my best friend. His brown eyes widen in shock, with questions dangling in them like a treat waiting to be devoured. "I really don't. She contacted me via Instagram."

"And?"

I shrug, setting the glass down, my mind on her. Everything has been on her for the past few hours, since she first sent me a message. It took me ages to respond, but now that I have, I'm hooked. I'm a fish caught in her net and all she has to do is pull me in.

I don't know how to deal with this.

"She's done a number on you," Mikael observes from his seat.

I want to refute his comment, but I can't because he's right. She has. And as much as I'd like to deny it, I can't. This woman has me in her grasp and I have no way of freeing myself.

There is something magnetic about her, something that pulls me in. I wish I can put a finger on it, to pinpoint exactly what this woman has done to me, but I can't.

Perhaps it's her innocence. Her sweetness. Having a submissive who's experienced is one thing, but having a woman who's new to this world kneel for you is more powerful than anything a Dominant can experience.

"Tell me," my best friend questions again.

"I have invited her to play out a scene with me. She's new. Brand-new to this world, this life." I can hear the wonder in my voice. That need to command her, to take her sweetness and watch as she unravels under my touch.

"And has she accepted?"

"Not yet. I had to leave my phone in the locker."

He nods at my response, knowing the rules. I'm itching to go out there, to see her message waiting for me, but I'm too wound up. I can't be with her until I've calmed the fuck down. It's not like me to be so out of control. My nerves are alive, sparking with electricity at the thought of seeing her.

"So why didn't you stay home? Talk to her, convince her to come down here with you on Friday, or meet here," Mikael says with a smile.

"I need a scene to calm myself down, something with an

experienced sub." I lift the glass of whiskey to my nose, inhaling the sweet smell. In one gulp, I swallow the whole lot, the burn trickling down my throat.

"Perhaps that's a good idea. I've never seen you so… I don't know, you seem different." He analyzes me like he always does. Seeing everything I want to hide, he's an expert at picking someone apart, finding their weaknesses and noting their strengths.

"We need to find that asshole's daughter. I thought she might be here at Runway tonight, but you're right, Friday would be better."

"Why don't you take Heather home tonight, scene with her in your own dungeon? Then when you're done, you can drink yourself into a coma." Mikael chuckles beside me as he gestures for another drink. "I'll stay up here and see if our blonde appears with her friends. If she's clubbing around L.A. she'll most certainly head in this direction soon."

"We both need to find her, I can't leave you to do all the work, and besides the only thing on my mind right now, besides our missing blonde, is having a beautiful woman on her knees, spread open." I grit through clenched teeth. My jaw ticks with frustration.

"Gentlemen," a sultry voice coos from beside me and we both turn to find a stunning brunette dressed in a champagne-colored dress that scoops low between her ample cleavage. Her long dark hair hangs in a sleek curtain to the middle of her back.

"And you are?" I ask, berating myself at how rude I'm being. Even though I just barked out the question, she doesn't seem deterred.

"I'm Annalise, but everyone calls me Anna. Perhaps you gentlemen were looking to visit the lower level?" She smiles, and I note how beautiful she is. Shimmering blue eyes that remind me of a tropical ocean, clear and bright, her bee-stung lips are bright red, pouty and full. My eyes rake over her slender neck, noting the thin collar she's wearing, and I wonder if she's owned, or if she's just wearing it as a hint as to her proclivities.

With a gentle curve to her hips, she has an hourglass figure that would look amazing bound in a black silk rope, but nothing spurs me on to invite her downstairs to one of the scene rooms deeper inside the club.

"Well, Anna," I say, rising from my seat. "My friend Mikael was just saying how he'd love a scene this evening." I pat my friend on the shoulder, not meeting his inquisitive glare that I can feel burning a hole into the side of my head. He wants to know why after I just said I needed a scene, I'm going to leave him to it.

"Kian—"

"I'll see you tomorrow, mate." I don't wait for a response. Instead, I head out the doors. Two drinks and I can't stop thinking about having another. But there's something more that's bugging me, or someone I should say.

I grab my things from the locker and head out to the parking lot. Once I'm in the driver's seat, I pull out my phone and press the *home* button to unlock the device. There, sitting neatly on the screen, is my app with a bright red notification. She's responded. It's got to be her.

I tap the icon and find a message that I don't think twice about opening.

I'll do it. Give me my orders and I'll play along. I want to learn. I want you to show me this life.

MY FINGERS MOVE SWIFTLY OVER THE KEYS AS I TAP OUT MY response, my mouth breaking into a grin. My body thrums with anticipation, the same anticipation I'm going to bestow on the lovely mystery woman.

First order is for you to tell me your first name only, pet.

I WAIT WITH MY BODY TENSE AS I WATCH THE SCREEN. IT'S BEEN A long time since a woman has caught my attention as much as this beautiful stranger has. Her response is swift.

Roisin, but most people call me Rosie.

SMILING, I WONDER JUST HOW STUNNING SHE'D LOOK WITH SOME rose hued welts on her skin. My cock throbs at the image in my mind and I tap out my response.

Tonight I want you to lie naked on your bed, turn a lamp on, not the overhead light, and take a photo of yourself. I want to see you from the neck down.

I hit send and start the engine. Hastily, I make my way through the streets of Beverly Hills on the way to my Los Angeles home. The house I've made my sanctuary. Soon, I'll have the woman who's captured my attention in my own personal dungeon, but first, she'll be visiting Black Light to experience firsthand what it's like to be pleasured under my command.

My chest is light. My heart thuds with excitement, with the need to have her here right now, naked, posing for me on the floor of my dungeon. I want to see her smooth skin in the dimly lit space where I can bend her to my will.

Moments later, I'm pulling into the garage and killing the

engine. When I look at my phone once more, there waiting for me is a photo. Exactly as I requested and my cock thickens in my slacks.

She's slim. Her breasts are just about a handful, and her skin is white as snow. Porcelain. Just the thought of marking her makes my dick throb with want and need. She knows what's coming next. When I hit send, I smile once more.

ROISIN

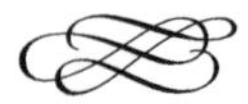

Good girl. x

I've been reading those same two words for the last eight hours. He sent them to me last night after I'd responded with my photo he'd asked for. Since then, I haven't heard from him. Needless to say, work has been difficult. I can't concentrate. He has been running through my mind. I still have no idea what he looks like, but deep down I feel this connection. A pull to a man I've never met face-to-face.

Staring at the blank screen before me, I watch the cursor blink. On. Off. On. Off. I recall his website, the image gallery that sat there in front of me as if taunting me. Each image beautiful in its darkness, but also offering a glimpse of something light, something freeing.

My phone vibrates with a message and I know immediately it's him.

Do you have a full-length mirror?

Frowning, I tap out a *yes* and hit send.

Today, I want you to send me another photo. This time, it will be in your bedroom. You'll turn off all the lights, then have two candles on either side of your kneeling form. No face, just head bowed, and you will be naked.

My heart races at the thought of sending him another photo. Last night was risky, I'd never done that before, but I'd asked him to show me this life and if I don't leap in with both feet, I'll never do it at all.

I type my response, but before I can hit send, another instruction comes from him.

I want you to go to La Perla this afternoon at 3pm. There will be an assistant by the name of Justine who will give you a dress. This is what you will wear on Friday if you choose to meet me. You will receive an email this evening from me for an event that I want you to attend. I want you in the black dress, along with a pair of black heels, four inches, nothing less. Your hair will be tied back into a low ponytail, and you will wear minimal makeup. Under your dress, you'll be draped in soft black lace panties with a bra to match. If you cannot get yourself a matching set, then let me know and I'll happily buy it for you. Am I understood?

My nerves are frayed by the time I reach the end of the message. I've always been nervous showing off my body because I've learned that men are bad. They do wicked things to pretty girls, when you're unique, different. And as much as I believe Master K won't hurt me, and we'll meet in a public place, I still can't damper the anxiety at another candid shot.

Last night it took all my courage to send the photo. I had swallowed down a shot of vodka before the time just to calm myself. But I couldn't stay still, thankfully he wouldn't have noticed it in the photo.

Another message vibrates on my phone and I know he's waiting for a response.

Am I understood?

I HAVEN'T OFFERED MY ASSENT YET BECAUSE I'M SCARED. FEAR holds me in its feral grip. But, I swallow it down and nod to myself.

Yes, Sir.

I CAN'T HELP SMILING WHEN I READ THE WORDS BACK TO MYSELF. I've never thought of myself as someone who'd give who I am so freely to another, but with him, there's a commanding presence that makes me want to do it.

I don't know what he looks like, but there's a flurry of excitement in my stomach. Turning back to my computer, I start typing up the review for the latest crime thriller I've been meaning to do for days.

Once that's sent off, I open my blog that's been dormant for a year and click on the new post option. I want to say something, to write it out, and I find my fingers flying over the keys easily as I work.

Words pour from my heart, appearing on the white page before me as my fingers bleed on the keyboard. With every word, and with each sentence, I feel lighter. I don't know if I'll ever make it public, but I allow myself to purge the anger from my past onto the screen.

Holding onto the past has always held me back. I realize I'm no longer that girl. I'm a new woman, I'm Roisin, and I'm about to become some dark Dominant's submissive. And even though that should scare the shit out of me... it doesn't.

My body is still thrumming with excitement. There's a storm raging within me, coiling in my stomach, tightening and threatening to strike at any moment. I know the moment it will is when I finally lay my eyes on the man who's captured me.

Not yet with his camera, but with his words.

"So, tell me about this job she's got you working on?" Greer questions, flopping onto the sofa beside me. My place is dimly lit, with candles on the fireplace, which has flames glinting in the wine glasses on the coffee table before us.

"It's this elusive photographer. The picture I sent you last night," I tell her, watching the recognition on her expression. "He takes them of these women who are naked and bound." I realize as I explain this, my voice is wistful. When I drop my gaze to the sofa, I twirl the material of the cushion between my fingers.

"And nobody knows what he looks like?"

Shaking my head, I reach for my drink. Lifting it to my lips, I take a long sip. The berry flavors of the red wine zing along my tongue, and I wonder what he likes to drink. Does he prefer beer, perhaps whiskey? I've been on edge all day. When I got the dress earlier, I couldn't wait to try it on. As soon as I got home, I slipped the material over my head and stared at my reflection, not recognizing myself. The sleek material is beautiful, stopping just above my knee. With the small scoop neckline, it only offers a small peek at my cleavage.

"What if he's some freaking pervert?" she asks, snapping me from the memory of how I felt wearing the gift he'll see on me tomorrow.

"I just think there's more to the story. To his story," I say, meeting her questioning gaze. Needless to say, the thought crossed my mind as well. But then, why would these beautiful women pose for him? I mean, if he's that weird, surely they wouldn't trust him.

"Would you pose for him?"

Would I? Yes.

"Possibly. He makes women look beautiful. What woman do you know who wouldn't want to look gorgeous? I mean, those images are just..." My words trail off because I can't explain it. Deep down I know it's not only the shadowed photos. It's the rope, the cuffs, the blindfolds.

"They're naked, Rosie, there's no way around it. He's a pervert, wanting to tie women up so they're helpless."

I know she's only looking out for me, and it would be the same way for me if she were to tell me she was thinking about doing something that could put her in harm's way, but I know Master K won't hurt me. I don't know how, but I trust that someone who lives in that particular lifestyle is careful with his actions.

A memory of the name I was given by the family I grew up with flits through my mind. A ghost from the past, one that haunts me on a daily basis. As much as I attempt to quell the thoughts, they still rear up unbidden. *Sinful devil child.* They believed I was bad, that I was evil.

"Sometimes it's what turns them on. There are people out there who have kinks most would shudder at. Who are we to judge them?" Gulping down my wine, I try to ignore the stare from my best friend. She's burning a hole through me with those big blue eyes and I don't want to look her way for fear of her seeing me. The real me that's hidden behind my floppy sweatshirts and glasses.

"Rosie." Her voice is tentative and I can no longer hide from her penetrating glare. "Are you? I mean, do you like *that* kind of thing?"

"What do you mean *that* kind of thing?" I question, my brows knitted together, furrowing at her in confusion. Her voice holds a slight hint of shock, but more so, it's the disgust that hangs heavy in her words.

"I just didn't know you liked being abused while having sex."

"That is not abuse," I bite back angrily, shooting up. I'm standing over the sofa, my body vibrating with anger and fear. For the first time in my life, I've been accepted, but now that she's found out about what I prefer sexually, I'm once again the outcast. "It's something that offers solace, calm, protection from abuse." My voice falters as I try to explain to someone who doesn't know what this lifestyle is like.

Granted, I haven't experienced it fully, but I've read enough to know there is no abuse in it. There's a beauty in the trust offered to a Dominant. I know what abuse is. I've lived through it.

There's an ache in my chest, reminding me that not everyone will understand. I don't care what people think of me, but for my best friend to judge me so harshly when all I wanted was support is painful to come to terms with. It's vastly different to the everyday person on the street.

All my life I've dealt with abuse of some sort. Whether it was at the hands of a foster father who was too touchy, or a man of the cloth who decided to use his religion to *show me God's way*. I never had a way of fighting back when I was younger, but this time, I have a choice. I won't let anyone debase me anymore.

"I didn't mean… I…" Greer's voice is small, stalling my thudding heart. "I just don't want you to get hurt. And I don't know much about it. Only what I've heard."

"There's nothing wrong with submitting yourself to someone, if you trust them. I've never told you about my past, well… the stuff I've been through makes being spanked by someone far less abusive. And it allows me the control to say no when I feel it's too much."

Her big eyes meet mine. There are tears glistening in them as she reaches for me. Pulling me into her arms, she holds me close and for the first time in a long while, I allow someone to care for me. Even though I haven't gone into detail about my teen years, I've offered her small snippets of the violence I'd witnessed. The pain of my past is something I've hidden for so long, not because I feel guilt, but I don't want to see pity when someone looks at me.

"I want to know, Rosie. We've been friends for a year now," she starts, nudging me gently to open up, but I can't. Not right now. I feel frayed, as if someone's taken the thread that held me together and tugged.

My mind flits back to *him* and I realize, while I was talking to him, I didn't feel the pain of my past, but an excitement for my future. This is what I want. I do want to learn from him, to allow him to teach and heal me. And somehow, I know he will.

"I can't talk about it right now, Greer," I tell her, sitting up. I take in her expression. I half expected pity, but there's none. "I want to try this."

"I just don't understand why having someone tie you up and slap you around is what you need," she says and I'm once more on my feet.

"I think it's time for you to leave. I can't fight with you right now."

She shoots up, watching me intently. "I'm not fighting. I just want you to think about it. I mean, how can a man want that?"

"Greer, please," I start. "I don't need your judgment."

Her mouth falls open, shock written all over her face. "I'm not judging. I just think it's stupid to want to give yourself to a man who gets off on hurting you."

"He won't hurt me." My voice becomes shrill with frustration. I hear it. She hears it. "This is my choice, Greer. I can't expect you to understand. Everyone has different tastes, needs, and this is mine. I'm sorry I brought it up."

"You know what, Rosie, if this is what you want, then go for it, but when he hurts you, don't come running back to me because all I'll do is tell you *I told you so*."

I watch her grab her purse and make her way to the door. With her hand on the doorknob, she doesn't look at me when she utters her goodbye and I'm alone in my condo once more.

I never expected people to understand this life. It's not something you tell anyone. I'm not even sure what I was expecting her to say, but it certainly wasn't that.

Sighing, I head into the kitchen. Placing the glasses in the sink, I grab my phone from the kitchen counter and head into my bedroom. I need to take the photo for Master K.

Silently, I strip off, taking in my appearance in the mirror. Slim hips, small breasts, and my pale skin. My long red hair hangs in waves down my back as I move about the room to light the candles.

When I turn off the overhead light, I finally get into position, but I'm shaking like a leaf in an autumn breeze. My heart is galloping a million miles a minute when I think about showing him my body. About exposing myself to him. I close my eyes, inhaling a deep breath, attempting to calm my erratic heartbeat.

I thought it might have been easier once I was here, kneeling, but it's not. A newfound respect for women who do this flits through me. It's not something I ever saw myself doing, but I know deep down it's what I need and want.

I fill my lungs once more, calming the thoughts, clearing my mind. I focus on the burning in my core, that twisting of excitement that tightens low in my stomach. The tingles that shoot through me. Every nerve in my body is alight with a current so fierce, I glance up, meeting my reflection, my cheeks flushed.

"You can do this," I tell myself. I want confidence in my body, in myself. I don't want to grasp at it a few times here and there. I want to grip it in a viselike hold and keep it with me. I nod. "You're beautiful. He will see it. He'll see past the pain. Do it, Rosie. Do it."

I sound crazy talking to myself, but it's the only way I lower my head and finally allow myself to forget who or what I am and offer up the item he wants.

I hold my phone in position as he instructed and I hear the harsh click of the camera. When I bring the device in view to inspect the image, I stare at it for a long while before I open the app, go straight to his profile, and send.

Since we've been speaking, he hasn't uploaded any new images to his account and I wonder if he's holding out. *Is he waiting to upload me? Will I be his new muse?*

Once the photo is sent, I rise and pull on my sleep shorts and a tank top. The room is warm this evening thankfully. I leave my phone on the bed while I get freshened up. Brushing my teeth, I note the flush on my cheeks in the mirror above the sink.

Slipping into bed moments later, I keep my phone close by in case he responds. I don't know if I want him to. I'm scared and shy. Nervous that he's seen me like that, but also intrigued to know if he liked it. I want to know if he thinks I'm pretty, beautiful, or just another girl.

I close my eyes, attempting to calm my erratic thoughts. Sleep is just stealing me when I finally hear the familiar vibration on the pillow beside my head. I should leave it for morning, but curiosity gets the better of me and I grab my phone.

Perfectly submissive. Tomorrow, we play.

And with those words in mind, I lie back and stare at the ceiling. Thinking back to Greer's reaction earlier, I wonder if she'll come around. If she'd even just listen to me, or give my feelings a chance.

Since moving here, she's been the only person I could really talk to. But now I feel as if she's closing herself off to me as well. If only life were easier. And if only people were more understanding of others' feelings and needs.

I close my eyes, hoping my best friend will accept my choices.

KIAN

The place I've called home for a while beckons as I pull up to the sleek gates of Runway West. There's another secret entrance for those who prefer stepping directly into Black Light, but I enjoy people watching as I walk through the main club.

It's the only place I can let go of all the stress of my job. And as I enter the secret club deeper inside the mansion, I can enjoy the scenes being played out. And every now and then, I find myself taking a submissive and devouring her body like she craves so much.

When my ex-wife walked out, I was lost. I didn't know what to do. That's when my partner invited me to join him. There is no way of knowing this place exists since it's in the basement of Runway, but for a select few, the scenes that await within are lascivious and unapologetic.

The car winds up the tree lined driveway toward the club. Between the tall trees, it appears as if it's a hidden treasure. Only those who are privileged enough to know about it can find the gem amongst the stones. About half way up the drive, I turn left down the almost hidden path that will take me to the lot where I need to be.

The mask that sits on the seat beside me is plain black. The theme for the evening is a masquerade. I've never been one to attend these because I find them tedious, but meeting the saucy little vixen who's been writing beautiful, erotic words to my photos has me intrigued. I want her to come. To see what she's missing out on. The pleasure I can bestow on her.

When I found her name, checked her background, I found the history of the two homes she was thrown into. She will soon know I've delved myself into her sordid background.

Roisin Nolan.

The girl who had been raised by a pastor and his wife until the age of sixteen. I don't know what happened exactly, but she was moved to a second foster home—not long after her birthday—where she spent two years until she turned eighteen and ran away.

She became a missing person that nobody looked for because she was alone in the world. But somehow, after the hardship she'd experienced, she has made a name for herself working for Plush Publishing. I sent her an invite to see if she'd actually take our flirting further than direct messages via our social media accounts.

Would she be brave enough to step inside my world and see where my inspiration comes from?

Exiting the car, I take in the Beverly Hills version of the club. The place drips with money. Two floors of utter decadence. Soft yellow light illuminates the monstrosity. I head toward the double doors where I can see a sweeping staircase just behind.

"Good evening, sir," one of the men at the door utters when I near them. One on either side of the entrance.

"Good evening." I nod. "I'm waiting on a guest," I inform him easily as I make way for more people entering the mansion.

Turning around, I glance at the parking lot, wondering if she's arrived as yet.

When my gaze lands on the lot, I find a woman with long, flowing red waves hanging down to her ass. *She's here.* I told her to wait outside, to find me on the left wing of the large doorway and there she is. Perfectly poised.

I make my way toward her car silently, taking in every inch of her.

A knee-length black dress hugs every curve of her frame. Thin straps snake their way over her shoulders, and a slim silver belt is tied around her torso just underneath her tits.

She moves and her dress shimmers under the light. As if she's hidden a million tiny stars in the dark material. Her head turns toward me. A soft gasp falls from plump lips.

"You scared me." Her voice is sweet and melodic. The mask she's wearing is beautiful, sparkling with diamanté along the edge, covering half her face.

"You came," I murmur, closing the distance between us. I don't touch her, though. As much as I'd love to, I fist my hands in my pocket, keeping the tingling in my fingertips at bay. For now. "We should go inside," I offer, and she nods shyly.

I can no longer stand not touching her, so I land a gentle touch to the base of her spine and lead her toward the entrance. We're granted access and find the security check point as soon as we step over the threshold.

"Good evening," the woman who's seated at the desk smiles. "We will need you to check in all electronic devices here. There will be a locker for you to safely store your belongings in," she tells us.

"Thank you," I offer a nod, lacing my fingers through Rosie's.

"Jarrod, can you open locker fifty-three for our two guests, please?" the woman, Amy as her name tag states, calls to the security. There's a click of metal farther down the hallway, and I turn to Rosie.

"Ready, sweetheart?" I question, my fingers finding the gentle curve of her back. A slight shiver travels over her body and I smile.

"Have a lovely evening, at Runway West," Amy tells me with a smile.

"Thank you, Amy," I respond. Turning, I guide Roisin toward the lockers. "We'll share a locker, your personal belongings will be in with mine, but please let me know if you want to leave throughout the event tonight. I'll escort you out."

"I understand." She smiles innocently, peering up at me with excitement in her pretty blue eyes. She's tempting. Utterly desirable and she's here because I invited her.

I pull the small door open, placing my phone inside. She follows suit with her purse. A small black and white one that I'm guessing holds her phone and whatever else women love to hide in those things.

Once I've shut the door, I take her small hand in mine. "Please, don't be scared. Nothing can happen unless you want it to." I assure her before I lead her toward the doors that await us. She's agreed by arriving, but soon, she'll see so much more than I'm certain she's even imagined.

The large space we step into is all marble and glitter and the staircase has been split into two, either side of a large foyer that houses a beautiful table with glass top. The black iron ornate railings line the stairs, where large floor-to-ceiling mirrors grace the walls.

A heavy crystal chandelier hangs from the high ceiling, shimmering with golden light. Everything is a cream marble with decadence oozing from every inch of the entrance. I head toward the ballroom. The space is large, with an ornate oval dome ceiling, a low hanging crystal chandelier, and the two main walls lined with glass doors that lead off onto a surrounding balcony.

People are mingling, soft chatter along with the music that's vibrating through the speakers. I can feel the excitement and trepidation that's skittering through the woman beside me and I wonder just how much she can take.

Since the dress code was black tie, everyone we pass are in their finest. Shimmering dresses and expensive tuxedos are all the eye can see.

"This place is incredible," she smiles as I lead her over to one of the balconies. I want to take her down to Black Light right now, but she's new, and taking it slow will be best for her to get accustomed to the club.

"It is." Agreeing with her, I stop on the balcony, allowing her to look out over the lush gardens that are only lit by sparse lamps. There's a swimming pool not far off, with a pool house I'm sure could tell some secrets of its own.

"I'm intrigued." She smiles up at me. Big blue eyes the color of a tropical ocean peek up at me, threatening to drag me into their depths. And I want to dive right in. To drown inside her, learning all about this petite redhead who's barreled into my life.

"Intrigue is good." I turn away from her once more. There's a fragility to her. As if she can break at any point. She's not much shorter than me in her heels, so when she stands beside me, I glance directly into her blue eyes, taking in her fiery locks.

She reminds me of those images you'd see of mermaids as a kid. Long flowing waves of hair with sharp features and a small button nose. Her eyes are wide, and I know that once she takes off her mask, she'll be a siren beckoning me to my death.

"Tell me, why my photos?" I ask, keeping my tone neutral, calm, and reserved. Most of the images she's chosen to use were of my BDSM scenes. The women are helpless, bound, blindfolded, some in the throes of passion. Lost in subspace where I take them, giving them pleasure beyond their imagination.

"They captured my attention because I've been wanting to try what I see in them. I've just never had anyone show me." Her confession is quiet, her voice dropping low, and I wonder if she's shy or ashamed for wanting to be spanked, perhaps even whipped. To be tied to a bed and forced to come over and over again.

The thought, the image of her submitting to me in that way, has my cock straining in my slacks. Two people stroll through the garden, heading toward the pool house, and I watch them for a moment before I turn to her.

"You want to be dominated?"

She nods.

"I want you to answer me, Rosie. I need to hear you say it. Your voice is your power. Remember that." I reach up, tapping my finger on the side of her forehead.

"Yes, I want to be dominated, sexually," she rasps. Her tone is heavy with need. She wants this and I don't want to deny her, but something tells me this girl has so many more layers to unravel before I can fully unleash myself on her.

"And how well do you take orders?"

"I can be obedient." Her voice lifts with confidence. She doesn't look at me. Instead, her eyes are glued to my shirt. I can tell there are a million and one thoughts racing through her mind right this second.

"You realize that if you're not you'll be punished."

It's not a question, but she responds with a nod. My body is vibrating with need to take her right here on the balcony. Not giving a fuck what people think. But I offer her my arm instead. She loops hers through mine, and I lead her into the ballroom.

It's filled up since we walked in, but we don't stay. We make our way toward the entrance to Black Light, the basement where the real show is.

"Where are we going?"

"You'll see." There's a lilt of warning in my voice. She can back out, I won't be angry. This is not for everyone. I've seen women race from watching a scene play out, even though they were adamant they could handle it. Granted, some men are more sadistic than others.

At the bottom of the private staircase we come to the final door and I pull on the lever. A soft click sounds and we're led into the inner sanctum. There's another security desk to our right with a man seated behind it.

He glances up, offering a small nod. "Member or guest?"

"Member of the D.C. club," I tell him easily. "Master K." Offering my scene name allows him to check the member list to ensure I'm not some stranger who's just walked in.

He taps the iPad a few times then nods. "And the lady?" he questions when he lifts his eyes from the screen.

"She's my guest." My gaze glances over the redhead, and I smile at the way she quirks her mouth playfully. "Rosie Nolan."

A few more taps and he nods in agreement. Her name will of course be there because I had sent it through for tonight. I know the procedure. My hand finds the base of her spine, leading her toward the window only a few feet from the security desk.

"This is quite a process," Rosie whispers up to me.

"They need to ensure anonymity and safety."

"Good evening, Master K." I recognize the girl from the D.C. club. Her long blonde hair has been pulled back into a tight bun and her big brown eyes are framed by small black glasses.

"How are you, Bianca?"

"I'm good. You'll love the new club, it's exquisite. Have you checked in all your electronics upstairs?"

I nod. "Yes, everything is in the locker."

She smiles then, a sweet innocent one, but I know she's played in D.C. before.

I release Rosie, pulling out my wallet. I find my membership card and hand it to Bianca. She lowers the lights, a soft purple glow, and that's when the name 'BLACK LIGHT' is illuminated on the front of the plain white paper.

Beneath the name are the words *Membership ID* along with the numbers I'd been given when I signed up. Each member has a specific combination. Bianca taps the screen of her tablet, then raises those pretty browns to mine.

"And your guest?"

"This is Roisin Nolan," I tell her, gesturing for Rosie to step forward.

Bianca hands her the form to fill in and sign. "Just sign this, initial each of the pages, and I'll need an ID for you, please."

Rosie takes the forms and the pen offered. Silently, I watch her initial the pages. RN. Her flowing script reminds me of a flowery pattern as she scrawls it with her left hand. It's said that creatives are all left-handed. Somehow, I believe it too.

The non-disclosure agreement for any guest and member of Black Light is airtight. It's there to ensure that what happens behind those doors stays there. Nothing leaves Black Light, and that's why there's so much security. The three partners who started this place have made a killing. The idea is genius, and what they offer, you can't get anywhere else.

Rosie finishes up signing her name and hands it back to Bianca. Then, she takes out an ID card that's about the size of her credit card. I know who she works for. Even though I know she's media, there's something about this woman I know I can trust.

At least, I hope so.

"And you'll need a stamp as well," Bianca informs my guest. "Just on the inside of your wrist, please."

Rosie nods, offering her arm palm up and I can't stop myself visualizing her presenting a whip, flogger, or any other toy to me. A smile plays on my lips, quirking at the innocence of this girl. Bianca presses a stamp to her wrist, which is barely noticeable.

The black light ink offers a discreet mark.

"Please remember, there is no technology inside. That includes phones, or any devices that can record. Unless of course it's medical, but that is the only allowance."

"I understand." Rosie smiles, a soft blush on her cheeks, and even in the purple light, I see her elegant beauty shine through.

"Master K," she says as we reach the entrance. She peeks up at me. There's an innocence in her gaze that makes me want to dive into those blue pools and drown in them, in her. "Thank you for the invite," she says finally with a sweet smile.

"Call me, Kian, sweetheart," I tell her with a smile. "And it's my pleasure," I respond, leaning in. I allow my mouth to find the shell of her ear, then whisper, "It will soon be all yours to experience."

With that, I head toward the doors that slide open and allow us into the main area of Black Light. It's far more opulent and over the top than the D.C. club, but it's just as generous on the exquisite furnishings.

The music is a gentle hum that resonates through me as Rosie snakes her arm through mine, pulling herself closer to me. I wonder if it's fear, or the need to be near me. Either way, I don't care. It's been a week of flirtatious chats, but now that she's in my den, I'm about to show her just how rabid I can be.

The lighting adds a soft warmth to the entire area. People are already mingling, their voices low and whispered. We make our way to the bar, where a few men are attempting to entice a lady to allow them to play a scene, I'm sure.

"This is..." Roisin utters in wonderment. Her eyes are wide as saucers as she takes in the space.

The barman appears just then and I place an order for a sparkling water with lemon for Rosie and a bourbon for me. Handing her the glass, I lift mine and sip it slowly as I watch her over the rim of the tumbler.

"Let's get a table," I offer, gesturing to one of the booths where we can sit down, soak in the atmosphere, and then I can show her the rest of the scenes that I know would be happening right before our very eyes.

ROISIN

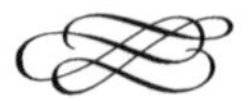

The club is beautiful, breathtaking. There are women who are dressed demurely, and some are dressed provocatively, but each of them are with a man. A Dominant. My eyes dart around in excitement and a hint of fear. Is this something I can do? I came here tonight to experience it, to allow Kian, or Master K, to show me what this life entails.

Perhaps it isn't for me. Maybe it's something I'll never do again, but I owe it to myself to try. He offered me an escape, and that's what I need. There were many times over the last day since his invitation arrived that I wanted to refuse. Tell him that this isn't going to work, but I couldn't bring myself to say it.

Instead, I agreed and now here I am.

"You're so quiet," he says in that deep, rough baritone. The rumble of it is like a warm blanket, thick and heavy, keeping me safe in the dead of winter.

"I'm just nervous. The idea of what's going to happen tonight is extremely new to me." My honesty causes him to smile. A crinkling at each corner of his eyes makes him look young and there's a quirk to his mouth. It lifts at the corner, offering me a boyish smile.

"Everything is new to someone for the first time, but trust me, darling"—he says, reaching for my hand—"you'll be just fine."

I nod, lifting the glass with my free hand and taking a long gulp. The cool liquid does nothing to quench the thirst inside me. And I realize it's not what I need, there's more than just a need for a drink, it's the yearning to experience.

"Can we... I mean... is there more?" I question slowly, my nerves once again frayed at the edges at what I'm about to find. The area we're in looks like a normal bar, but I'm sure more decadent secrets hide behind the velvet curtains.

"Of course." He rises, buttoning his suit jacket. He's dressed immaculately. The dark suit that seems to be tailored for him hugs his tall, broad frame. The crisp white shirt he wears beneath it looks painted on. I know his day job is something he told me he won't talk about, but that only piques my curiosity.

Once again, he takes my hand in his, engulfing it in his warmth, and we make our way through the club. There are small alcoves where couples are sitting, some chatting, others drinking, and a few where the women are seated on the laps of the men.

He leads me toward the drapery and my heart catapults into my throat making it difficult to swallow. My nerves are getting the better of me, and a flurry of hummingbirds find flight inside my stomach making me tremble.

When we step through, the light dims and the music turns into a sensual, sultry beat that seems to travel through me. We reach an area that's open to view. There are scenes playing out around us and I'm not sure where to look first because I want to see everything all at once.

One in particular catches my attention. Two men are cocooning one woman, her legs splayed over their respective thighs as one man's hand disappears under her dress. She's in ecstasy. The show they put on causes me to squeeze my own thighs together.

Heat floods my veins. My panties are dampening as we move

deeper into the debauchery that's taking place for all to see. A woman is bound to a black leather bench, her body naked to the men and women who have their eyes glued to her.

With each cry that falls from her lips, the man who's spanking her with a small wooden paddle tells her to count. From a distance, you might wonder if she's crying out of pain, but somehow, I believe it's from the sheer twisted pleasure he's doling out on her body. He reaches for a wand, a vibrator that I've heard works wonders, and places it on her pussy.

She starts shaking wildly, but the man orders her to hold back. She's not allowed to come. Her pleas are loud and echo around us. Kian moves closer to me, his hand snaking its way around my hips, gripping one painfully, but I don't whimper. I'm too entranced by the show.

He shifts behind me then, holding both my hips, pulling me closer to him. That's when he presses his hardness against my ass and I do whimper.

His mouth is at my ear that instant. "If you want anything we do here to stop at any point, you call out red. Do you understand me?"

"I understand," my murmur comes along with the woman crying out for more.

"Do you like watching, pet?" he questions, his hot breath fanning over my cheek, down my neck. His hands wander between my thighs, lifting my skirt until it's bunched up in front. Deft fingers find the wet spot in my panties and he growls in my ear.

"Yes, I do." I don't recognize my own voice when I respond. It's raspy, heavy with need so fierce I feel like I'm burning up from the inside out. "Please," I beg. Me and the woman I'm staring at both plead for more, for less, for something we need, but we don't know what. Only the men who are toying with us like puppets know.

Kian snakes his fingers under my panties, the material already sodden with arousal. My eyes flutter closed, but he murmurs in my ear, "Open your eyes, watch her."

I do. I focus on her, but the way he presses my clit, circling it with his index finger has my knees buckling.

Kian holds me up, but once again whispers in my ear, "Do not come."

It's an order.

One I can't deny. I can't disobey him. I try to think of something else, something other than what I'm watching and feeling. He dips two fingers into me, inside my warmth, the slick juices coating his fingers.

Moans fall from my mouth the same time as cries fill my ears from my partner in pleasure, the woman before me. She's so close, and I'm right there with her. Beside her in the pleasure that's racing through my veins like poison threatening to steal me away.

Her Dom orders her to come the same time Kian growls in my ear. "Do it. For me." Four simple words unleash an orgasm that sucks me into its depths and I can no longer stand. He's pressing me up against his body. My head falls back as I cry out my release.

I'm unaware of everything around me. Waves crash through me and I'm flying. His fingers are pulled away and he brings them to my lips, painting me with my own sweet, musky release.

"Such a good girl," he says in awe. His words bathe me in warmth and excitement.

When I open my eyes again, he spins me around, his mouth crashing on mine as his tongue laps at the arousal coating my lips. A growl, feral and basal, vibrates through his chest and into me. He devours me in that moment. A hungry kiss that steals every breath I have and replaces it with his.

I lose time.

I forget my name.

And when he pulls away, I mourn the loss of his lips on mine, but I'm more turned on than I've ever been.

"That was amazing," I breathe, peeking up at him. I can feel the blush on my cheeks as heat spreads down my neck over my breasts. My nipples are peaked, pushing against the soft material of my bra.

"You're amazing." His words are dripping with want, with a desire that seems to light his blue eyes with a flame. And I find that I'm the moth heading straight into the light. The one thing that scares me most is how badly I'm about to get burned.

"Do people always do that? I mean, when we… When you take me, will they…"

"There are private rooms. We don't have to—"

Shaking my head, I interrupt him. "No, I do want to. I'm just not sure I want to be watched by others." My shyness rears its head, which earns me a smile.

Kian brings his fingers to his mouth, then hums in pleasure as he cleans them. "You certainly didn't mind while we stood beside four other men." He winks, gesturing to the people now moving off to the next show.

"They couldn't see us." I gasp in shock. He's right, I was so lost in pleasure, I don't know for sure if they didn't see us.

"I'm teasing you, love." He leans in, pecking the tip of my nose with a kiss. "Ready for the next show? Or are you ready to play?"

I honestly don't know. Am I ready?

"Come," he says, taking me farther into the club. We pass more shows, but most of them are only getting started, people kissing, kneeling, and some in various states of undress. When we finally reach a hallway with doors running along the left side, my breath catches.

This is it.

Kian leads me to one that's ajar. We step inside and find it empty. There's a large four-poster bed, along with a big wooden X against one wall, and two benches similar to the one the woman was bound to.

Also in the room is a chest of drawers and I wonder what exactly it can hold. What toys and implements are hidden in it. I make my way farther into the room, taking in every inch. Once I've fully taken everything in, I turn to Kian, who's leaning against the closed door.

He's taken off his mask, and I follow suit. His blue eyes are glued to me, watching my every move. I walk over to the wall where the numerous whips and floggers hang. There are leather ones that give off the scent of the material. Foreboding and heavy.

Allowing my fingers to trail them, I shiver at the thought of how they feel when used on naked flesh. The silence in the room is thick with excitement. My heart hammers against my chest in rhythm. A melody that only I can hear, ringing in my ears. I turn to Kian, wondering if he can perhaps hear it, but he makes no sign to move or say anything.

"Are these what you'll use on me?" I question, lifting a crop from the hook. I've spent the past two nights researching all the toys. Everything a Dominant would use, and some have scared me, but others have intrigued me.

"Yes, I'll spank you a few times, use the crop and if you enjoy that, we'll see what other toys I can use. It will be a gentle toe dip into my world," he responds. "Remember, pet, you do have a safe word. If anything is too much, or if you're feeling scared at all, you call out *red.*" He tells me seriously. His face a picture of confidence and desire. The emotions swim in his gaze as he watches me. "Do you understand?"

"Yes, I understand. Red." I utter the word, tasting it on my tongue. I'm in control. My body is still trembling, but knowing I'm the one who can stop this at any point makes me less fearful and more intrigued.

"You are safe here. A submissive has the power to halt a Dominant at any point with one simple word." This causes the corner of his mouth to tilt upward into a grin. "It may seem like I'm in charge, but I can't do anything you don't want."

"I understand, thank you," I whisper shyly, lowering my head in an attempt to hide from him. Making my way over to the bed, I trail my fingertips over the sheets. He is still leaning against the door, when I meet his hungry gaze.

"Take off that dress for me." His voice is a vibrating rumble.

I shiver at the order, unsure of taking my clothes off, even though he's already seen the photo I sent him.

"Roisin, I suggest you obey. Unless we walk out of here and go have a drink?" His brow quirks, causing me to shake my head.

Nervously, I slip the material over my shoulders, shuffling it down my thighs until I'm standing in only my panties and bra. I set aside my shoes, along with my folded dress.

"Everything."

I know he means my underwear, so I close my eyes, silently willing myself to be strong. My stomach is a flurry of butterflies and hummingbirds.

My trembling fingers move for the clasp of my bra, undoing it, letting the straps slip from my shoulders. Once I'm standing before him in only my panties, he moves. Striding toward me, his gaze falls to my body. There's a scar he'll see on my leg from the one night I fought back against my attacker. He pulled a knife and I'll forever live with the memory.

"What happened?" he questions, taking me in.

"Life."

My one-word answer earns me a nod. He doesn't say anything more. His hands reach for me, spinning me around. With one hand on my back, he makes me bend at the waist, my breasts squashed against the mattress.

"You want to be spanked with a crop, pet?"

"Yes, Sir," I respond, hoping I get it right. I want this. I need it.

"It's Master, or Master K when we're in a scene," he says.

"Yes, Master."

"Good girl," he utters. "You'll count. Ten swats, five on each cheek. Can you handle that?"

"I can handle anything you give me, Master."

He deftly pulls my panties down my hips, leaving them at my

thighs. I gasp when his hands grab my ass cheeks, squeezing them, pulling them apart. The blush of embarrassment that warms my face is red hot.

"Such pretty little holes," he says with pride lacing his tone. He continues to toy with both cheeks, causing me to whimper and moan. He massages me for a moment longer before releasing me and lifting the crop.

He doesn't warn me. I don't expect him to. When he brings down the leather implement, it stings only slightly.

"One." Swat.

"Two." Swat.

"Three." Swat.

"Four." Swat.

"Five." Swat.

He gives me a moment to breathe, then continues to ten. The flesh on my ass burns, but the sensations that trickle through my body are otherworldly. That makes me wonder how good it would feel with a flogger, or whip, or even a cane.

"You're such a good girl for me," he says, helping me to stand. He pulls my panties up and steps back. "How do you feel?"

I meet his imploring blue gaze and answer honestly. "Needy, Master."

"Is that pretty pussy wanting to be filled with my thick cock?" he taunts. I nod.

I want nothing more than to be fucked hard right now. To be impaled on his erection. To scream his name. I want it rough, almost violent, but he just nods.

His fingers probe me against the material of my panties, delicately, as if I'm breakable. Maybe I am. Perhaps after all these years of fighting, surviving, I want to finally let go of all the control and let someone else be there for me.

"Gently, pet," he hums across my skin. It's as if he's all around me and inside me, not physically, but mentally. "Have you ever had a blindfold on?"

"No, Master," I mewl at the ministrations of his digits on my nipples. He pulls and tugs on them until my knees once again buckle. What is it about this man that makes me so weak?

His control.

His dominance.

"Then tonight, I'm going to cover your eyes. I'm going to make you feel everything," he promises, stepping away and toward the chest of drawers. Pulling the top one open, he finds what he needs and returns to me with a soft black piece of material that he places over my eyes.

"What is this going to achieve?" I question, knowing I'm out of place for asking, but he doesn't call me out. I didn't use the title he asked me to call him.

"It allows you to let go. You're tense, nervous, but once I'm done with you, there'll be no doubt in your mind."

He guides me to the bed, allowing me to lie flat on my back. With silent movements, he takes my wrists and binds them to the metal headboard, sending a shiver of anxiety through me.

"Calm. I'm here," he assures me, and I know he noticed my trepidation against the bindings. "Remember, there's nothing here to hurt you. If you feel you can't you tell me. Do you remember your safe word?"

"Yes, Master," I whimper, breathing through the tension. Then he continues the same thing below with my ankles. My legs spread wide, opening to him and his hungry stare.

I feel it.

I feel his eyes on me, roving over every inch of my skin.

"You're an incredible young woman, pet," he compliments me, but I don't respond. I never learned how to take compliments. Most were lies. Used against me when I believed in them, so I steeled myself.

A harsh swat lands on my bare thigh, causing me to jolt and cry out in pain, the sting trailing its way over every part of me.

"When I say you're beautiful, you say *thank you, Master.* Do you understand me, pet?"

"Yes, Master. Thank you, Master," I whimper, still reveling in the pained pleasure of the spank on my leg.

"Good girl."

I hear a shuffle, but seconds later it stops and I'm in complete darkness and silence. The strange thing is, I can't move, but I feel free. Confusion settles in my mind as I lie there, open to a man I've only known for a week.

A gentle melody starts and I realize there are speakers all around the room. The song that plays is instrumental, calming, yet there's an urgency building gradually. Suddenly, a featherlight touch trails over my arms, down toward my breasts, and farther still to my stomach.

It stops at the waistband of my panties, and I finally breathe again. And that's when Kian speaks. "Time to play."

KIAN

There's a slight shiver that travels over her body, making my cock throb. I love watching how women whimper and tremble. Her slight frame is a wet dream come to life. And I can't for the life of me understand how she's all alone in this world.

Perhaps her past was too much for her to handle, too much for her to allow someone in, to trust. I don't understand why she wants this life when something inside her is so clearly shattered. The question is, how badly has someone hurt her? The thought makes me livid, vibrating with rage.

There are slight scars, almost gone, but still a faint reminder of what she has been through. Was it the foster father who did this? Or was there another man in her life that inflicted damage on the beauty I can't drag my gaze away from? I should've delved deeper into her past. But I wanted to learn about her from those plump lips, rather than stalking her like a man obsessed.

Her eyes pleaded with me earlier as she watched me. Her gaze begged me not to look at her imperfections, but more to see who she is. And I do. I see her as a survivor. I'm intrigued. Since the first message to the first meeting, and now, as we play our first scene, I'm captivated.

The music that plays in the background is calming the rage at the thoughts of someone hurting her. Taking the feather, I trail it over her mound, causing her to cry out as it tickles along the sheer see-through material that hugs the lips of her cunt. She's utterly breathtaking. Every inch of her, and I vow to devour her like my last meal. I want to drink her in as if she were my sustenance.

I can see a thin strip of hair just above her clit, neat and tidy, just how I like the women I'm with. I place the feather beside her, lifting the cat o' nine tails flogger, and allow it to lick her flesh. Again and again. The soft hue of pink that now marks her skin in beautiful patterns make me impossibly harder. The porcelain skin I've marked is begging for more, her hips rise and fall, her mewls are like music to my ears, and I'll gladly listen all day.

"Master, please," she begs, her back arching beautifully. She's a masterpiece and I can't wait to capture her with my lens. To steal her in moments of bliss and hold onto them.

I don't respond. I allow the music and the leather to take her into a mindless state. Lifting the flogger, I bring it down over her flat stomach, earning me a delicious whimper. Soft, melodic, even better than any song I've ever heard.

Blush pink welts start to turn red and rise up on her smooth flesh, pretty lines from the flogging. Her body writhes in pleasure, her plump lips part on moans and pleas, and the material of her sheer panties is soaked by the time I drop the implement to the floor.

I want to fuck her. To take her hard and fast, but I also want her to beg. I untie her legs and wrists, then hover my body over hers. She fits beneath me like she was always meant to be there.

It's a strange feeling having a submissive so innocent and so damn pliable. Most of the women I've been with have already had experience. They've played scenes, but with Roisin, she's mine to break.

"Are you aching, pet?"

"Yes, Master," she whispers when my lips find her hardened nipple peaked, ready for me to devour. I suckle it into my mouth, my teeth grazing the bud, tugging it gently. The sounds she makes are like a drug. A fast hit of cocaine, something that slams into you and grips you in its feral claws.

"Tonight, you'll go home, but you will not come. Do you understand me?" My voice is rough and husky, filled with want. She's so beautiful, so fucking perfect, that my restraint is a barely there thread, pulled taut, ready to snap.

"I… I…"

"Don't make me spank you again," I warn in a no-nonsense tone.

"No, Master. I understand." She pouts, her lips pursed in frustration.

I move to undo the blindfold and I'm once again met with those big innocent eyes. This beautiful woman with her red hair and blue eyes, is a contrast to my ex-wife in every way. And she's nothing like any other submissive I've ever been with. She's unique.

"Come sit with me," I tell her, turning to the large armchair in the corner. I settle, waiting for her to rise on wobbly legs. I know she's turned on, needing a release, but I want to test her obedience. Orgasm denial is something I've used before, and it's offered me a glimpse into the mindset of a woman. Is this something she can endure, or will she break and finally offer herself the release I wouldn't?

She pads toward me, her tits bouncing with every step, which only further hardens my dick. I pat my lap with one hand, which she smiles at, settling herself on my thighs.

"Tell me about these," I question, trailing a fingertip over the marks on her body. The silence that greets me is confirmation that she's been through far worse than I could've imagined. I feel the tremble that shoots through her small frame when I press down on one closer to her cunt. "Tell me."

After a gentle sigh, I know she'll give me what I want. "I-I didn't have an easy life growing up," she offers but doesn't meet my eyes. That's something that will need to change. I reach for her chin, turning her face toward me.

"When you talk to me, I want your eyes on me. Am I understood?"

"Yes, Master." Her response is quick, obeying my command to call me Master. "I grew up in two nasty foster homes. The first was when I was younger, and..." She grows silent and I know she must be in pain from recollecting it, but I need to know if she may have any triggers.

"Rosie, you don't have to tell me everything right now, but I need you to know, soon you will need to give me the truth. As I told you, honesty is key in this."

"I understand, Master." There's sadness in her gaze, and I have the urge to wipe it away. I trail my hand up her thigh, finding her core. My fingers circle her clit, taunting, eliciting a moan as I dip one long finger into her.

She's warm and wet. Her walls pulse around my digit. I can feel how close she is, just on edge. Her one hand grips my wrist. Her hips move against my hand as she attempts to ride my finger to her release, but I pull back before she can find euphoria.

"Why?" she questions, meeting my eyes.

"It's a test, sweetheart," I tell her. "I need to know if you'll obey."

"You know I will," she whines and I swat her ass harshly, causing her to yelp in surprise.

I pin her chin between my thumb and index finger, bringing her mouth to mine. Her lips mold to my own in a soft kiss. "I know you'll obey me on my simple commands like taking a picture, but this is more of a challenge. When you're needy for me, that makes it harder to obey. And from tonight, until we decide otherwise, all your orgasms belong to me."

"Yes, Master," she murmurs with a smile on her lips and I steal her mouth once more. Her tongue dips against mine tentatively, but when I tweak her nipple between my fingers, her kiss deepens and I revel in her flavor.

When I pull away, her breaths are shallow. Ragged and short. Need dances in her blue eyes and I smile. Making a woman so needy is an addiction. One I'll never tire of.

"Come, I will walk you to your car. I want you to message me as soon as you get home. Am I understood?"

"Of course, Master." Her words are soft, whispered for only me to hear.

"Good girl." Those two words uttered over her smooth skin causes her to shiver. She lifts her eyes to mine and gifts me a smile that stills my heart for a moment. There's so much innocence in her, so much beauty.

I tap her butt, causing her to stand.

"Get dressed, sweetheart," I order, watching her as she moves across the room. With every movement, her body catches the low lights and I can't drag my gaze away from her. I watch her until she's fully clothed and I'm no longer awarded a view of her perfect body.

I stand, shrug on my jacket, and move through the space, closing the distance between us. I pull her into my arms and plant a gentle kiss on her forehead.

"Tomorrow, you will come to my home. I want to see you in my dungeon."

"Yes, Master." And there it is. She's mine.

It's almost one in the morning, but I can't move. I've been sitting in my car watching her move through her condo. From what I can see, she's dressed in a large T-shirt that hangs off one shoulder. Her long fiery hair is pinned atop her head. She's sitting in the window seat of her living room, her nose in a book, and I wonder what she's reading.

I've turned into a fucking stalker, but after she drove away from Runway earlier, I couldn't let her go just yet, so I followed her to her condo. I feel that deepening obsession with her, and I know it's only because of her innocence. How new she is to this world.

With the moon hidden behind the clouds, a soft yellow light hangs from the street post, illuminating the garden at the front of her building. I watch in awe as she drops her head back, lengthening her neck, and as I'm about to leave her for the night, she drops a hand over her pert tits, down between her legs. She's unknowingly taunting me from the second floor of the building.

The soft light that sits above her goes off, casting her in silhouette. I can't stop myself. Lifting the camera, I snap a shot of her pulling off her sweater. The material falls from her hands and I imagine the *whoosh* sound as it drops on the bed. Then, one more of her tugging on a top, which hides her slim frame from my view.

Roisin is small, petite with a set of tits that make my cock hard. She tugs at the hair tie, allowing her long flowing fiery waves to hang down to her ass and I wonder if she's getting hot because, from my view, I see her turn on the overhead fan. The blades spin slow and hypnotic.

She slides the blinds closed completely and I'm no longer afforded a view of her beauty. The memory of her bare breasts have me salivating. My tongue licks my lips, tasting her in my mind. I'd give anything to be close to her right now, to inhale her, devour her beautiful body. I want to delve into her mind and root around on hands and knees to see what she hides.

My phone beeps, causing me to grab it, swiping my finger over the screen. A new notification glares at me with a taunting red dot. She's just posted something new. She has certainly intoxicated me, but it's also her filthy words that have drawn me even closer. I want to peel back layer by layer of her until she's nothing but a broken little toy in my hand, until all she wants and needs is me.

I want her as obsessed with me as I am with her.

With her using my images as inspiration for those beautifully erotic verses, I wonder just how she'd feel being the one in the photos. Tomorrow night, or rather, later tonight, I'll make her my muse as she has made me hers. There's a tether between us, it's pulled taut, but never snapping. I won't allow it to.

After our scene, I should've offered her more, to take her to dinner, or for drinks, but I knew my restraint was barely there. I would have never been able to let her go without fucking her. And if there's one thing I've learned, anticipation is key. I hold my phone in my hand as if it connects me to her physically.

How I wish I had her kneeling for me right now. Her head bowed in the shadows of her bedroom while I capture her with my lens. Opening her profile once more, I read the words on screen.

Her body quivers and trembles.
It's what he does to her as he watches.
Dark souls, dirty needs.
What will you do when you find her?

MY HEART SLAMS INTO MY RIBS WITH BOTH CONFUSION AND excitement. I haven't been this intrigued by a woman in a long time. Needing to know her, to learn who she is behind those big blue eyes and those filthy words.

I open the direct message window, staring at it for a long while trying to figure out how the fuck I'm going to approach this without her running scared. One scene doesn't give me the right to lay claim over her, but I want to. I fucking need to.

I tap out a message. An order.

Tomorrow, I want you in red lingerie. You'll leave your hair in waves and you are to meet me at the below address. Do not wear anything over your underwear, except a coat. If you do not have one, I will purchase it for you. I want you in four-inch heels, red to match the lingerie and that beautiful fiery hair. You will be at my home at 8pm and expect to stay over.

I GLANCE UP AFTER HITTING SEND. LIFTING MY CAMERA, I SNAP HER through the window. She's in the bedroom, staring out the window, and I wonder if she can sense me. Am I inside her as much as she is in me?

I put people like me behind bars. Fucking obsessive stalkers. My gaze trails up to her window once more before I make my decision. I want to teach her, but I also want to claim her. I can't explain why, but I will. She will submit to me and me only. No other man will come near her because I'll have her as mine.

A response comes immediately and I smile at my new pet.

Yes, Master K. I'll be there, in anticipation.

MY FINGERS FLY OVER THE KEYS, AND I HIT SEND.

Good girl.

THEN I START MY CAR AND PULL OUT ONTO THE ROAD. IT'S TIME TO go home and prepare the room for her. I've always been excited when I had a shoot coming up, but this is so much more. And I can't wait to unravel her.

ROISIN

It's been less than twenty-four hours and all I can think about is him. How his hands touched me, stroked me, and made me wet and needy. The low timbre of his voice that barreled through me in that thick accent I recognize as Scottish.

Last night, his message was a welcome distraction from my thoughts. Knowing tonight I'll be with him again, I can't get myself to settle down and work.

I never knew a man could hold so much power, but Kian did. He exuded it like a cologne, and I wanted to bask in it for days, weeks even. When he asked about my past, about the first man who had taken me in as a daughter, I couldn't offer him the truth.

Not because I didn't trust him.

But because I didn't want him to see me like a broken toy.

Deep down I feel shattered, but last night, being bound to the bed, feeling the gentle whisper of a feather on my skin, the heat of Kian's gaze and touch, I was whole for the first time in years. I finally found my center, and it was at the hands of a man who wants to spank me, bind me, and blindfold me.

I make my way into the kitchen and grab my coffee mug from the dishwasher. Once it's on the counter, ready for the boiling water, I push the kitchen window open, allowing the cool morning breeze to filter through.

I think about our scene, about everything we did, and I wonder if there'll come a time when he'll tell me it's over. I don't want that day to come. Instead, I want to experience everything he's offering.

Submission is a gift.

One I want to offer him.

Last night proved he isn't a crazy person, he's a man who may hold secrets, but he's also someone who needs this life to feel whole. The same as me. I want it all and I want it with him.

I race to the bedroom, grab my phone, and open his profile. There are no new images, but I scroll down, trying to find one that fits, and when I find it, I quickly save and crop it.

Hitting the new button, I select the picture and type out my caption.

It's your touch burned into me
It's your kiss scorched on my skin
And it's your words that are emblazoned in my mind
Take me away, Master, take me higher, take me deeper,
Show me the light...

It's a message. One directed to him, asking him, pleading with him to offer me that once more. Something I've never wanted, but something I always needed—the strength I find in my submission, the confidence in my body, and the need to please him, pleases me.

I know this wouldn't make sense to anyone else. But to me, it's exactly right.

My phone rings, jolting me from the thoughts of Kian, and I see my boss's name on the screen.

"Good morning," I answer, hoping she's not calling about the article, but I know that's wishful thinking.

"Rosie, I was hoping you'd have some news for me." She sounds more hopeful about this than I feel. I don't want to out Kian. His privacy is important to him. But this is my job on the line, and I have to come up with something to give her or she's going to fire me. I can just tell.

"Well, I have an interview with him tomorrow morning," I tell her, hoping with all my heart that Kian would allow me a moment to ask him questions.

"Great news! I look forward to the email from you in the afternoon then," she tells me before hanging up without waiting for my response. My nerves prickle at the thought of delving into his mind, attempting to learn more about the man behind the lens. I have to do it, but how am I going to tell him?

It's almost time. I've been sitting in the car, staring up at the mansion that awaits me. There's nothing calming about it. Large, foreboding, just like the man himself. The numbers on the clock tell me there's another two minutes before my cut off. I start the engine and pull up to the enormous metal gate. Pressing the buzzer, I wait until I hear a soft crackle on the other side, and then I hear him.

"Gates will open, park on the left of my car." That's all and then the gates are opening. As I inch forward, I'm met with the lit up home I'm about to enter.

As soon as I'm out of the car, I make my way toward the double wooden door that slides open as I near it. On the other side is Kian. He's dressed casually in a pair of black slacks. The shirt he's wearing is unbuttoned and I'm afforded a view of his beautifully toned torso.

"You're on time," he says appreciatively.

"I am." I smile up at him. The heels I'm wearing put me almost at his height, but there's still a few inches difference between us.

"Come in." He gestures to the inner sanctum of his home.

Stepping inside, I take in the entry hall that's brightly lit with soft fluorescent globes. There's a small table that holds a bowl filled with keys and other knickknacks, and a large painting that takes over one wall. The modern paint splattered on it is a mesh of deep blues and light grays.

"Can I take your coat?" Kian questions from behind me and I'm about to say yes when I remember what's beneath the coat.

"Maybe I should keep it on for now," I respond, turning to face him, my face hot with embarrassment.

"You are never to be shy in front of me, Roisin," he murmurs with seriousness in his tone. "Your body is perfect, beautiful, and if I want you walking around my house in nothing but your fucking heels, I'll order you to do it. And you know what you will do in return?"

I glance up, noting the way his eyes, normally blue, are so dark, they're they color of the night sky, but there's an expression on his face that tells me not to argue. "I obey?"

"Good girl," he coos in my ear. "You're learning." He allows me to keep the coat on, but I know it won't last long. I wonder if he's only appeasing me to make sure I'm comfortable here, alone with him.

He laces his fingers through mine and leads me into the living room, which is decked in black leather sofas and dark wood bookshelves along one wall. There's a large oak coffee table that sits on a white shag rug in the middle of the two sofas.

The walls are painted a dark gray, almost charcoal, reminding me of a stormy sky. The large fireplace that sits against one wall causes me to envision being fucked on the shag carpet on a cold winter night, curled up against Kian.

"Would you like a drink?"

"Yes, please." I turn to him as he saunters behind the small bar in the corner of the room. Following him, I settle on one of the stools and watch as he pours a large glass of white wine. He hasn't asked my preference, and I wonder if he knows how much I favor white over red.

He places the glass on the counter in front of me then pours a large shot of amber liquid into a tumbler.

"To us," he says, lifting his glass, clinking it against mine.

"Can I ask you something?"

"Anything, sweetheart." He smiles, swallowing the shot of whiskey before looking at me again.

I take a sip of my wine, allowing the alcohol to offer me some sort of courage, or nerves of steel to ask him, "Why me? There are many other beautiful women out there, but you want me here?"

The corner of his mouth lifts. "Because you're beautiful, and to be honest, your innocence calls to me," he tells me easily.

"And… you haven't photographed anyone since we started talking." It's not a question, but he shakes his head anyway.

"No, because I want to capture you," he promises.

And I know that wasn't meant in the way I'd asked. He doesn't mean he wants to take my photo. No, this man wants so much more.

"Then you should," I offer, hoping he'll read between the lines. I lift the glass to my lips once more and smile. His gaze lingers on my lips, watching as I lick the alcohol left from my sip.

"You're beautiful," he says. "Come." Offering me his hand, he pulls me to stand beside him, and I can't help smiling at how I fit into the crook of his arm as if I've been molded to his form.

He leads me through the long hallways until we find a door that's painted black. The gold doorknob shines under the ceiling lights.

"Is this your black room of pain?" I giggle, glancing up in time to find him rolling his eyes at my reference.

"Behave yourself," he groans, opening the door and allowing me to slip inside. When I do, my breath is caught in my throat. The space is beautiful. An open plan room with walls the color of charcoal. There are three small benches in one corner, the sight of them gives me shivers. I wonder if he'll bend me over any of them.

One wall is purely made of windows that overlook darkness and I wonder if there's a garden beyond. One I can't see in the darkness. He takes his time, tugging the curtains closed, and soon the glass is hidden by black drapery. The other walls are dark, with implements hanging on silver hooks. And in one corner are black cuffs hanging from the ceiling.

There's rope, whips, chains, and even a wooden cane in glass cabinets against the fourth wall. The room is calming, but there's an edge just beneath the surface that tells me there's pain to be experienced in here.

"Don't be scared, sweetheart," Kian says from behind me, startling me because I forgot he was even there.

"I'm not, I'm just…" I spin on my heel, taking in everything, the king-sized bed beckoning me with its black silk sheets, deep blue pillows, and the four posters I know are for binding me to.

"Let me calm you down." His voice coos from behind me. His hands are on my shoulders, tugging on my coat, ridding me of the offending item. Once it's hung on the rack, he turns toward me once more, his dark gaze drinking me in. There's desire swimming in his stare and I feel it right down to my bones.

"You know"—I start—"if there's something you can do to calm me down, you're not doing it currently."

"Oh?" He quirks a brow at me.

"You're looking at me like you want to eat me," I mumble and a chuckle slips from his lips. I realize my faux pax, and I blush furiously.

"I do want to eat you, sweetheart, but not in the way you'd

imagine. I'm not a monster out to capture the princess," he tells me earnestly. "I'm the man who wants to be with a beautiful woman, if she'll let him."

A smile breaks on my face. My chest fills with happiness when Kian cups my face in his strong hands and leans in as he plants a kiss on my lips.

"I think she'll let him."

He nods, steps back, and stares at me for a moment before ordering, "Turn, slowly."

I obey as excitement skitters down my spine, the need to please him tingling over my skin. I can feel the heat of his glare on my skin, the heels, lingerie, everything is done for him, because he asked me to. No. He ordered me to.

"Perfection."

He takes my hand and leads me over to the bed. I watch as he cuffs my wrists to the two posts at the foot end, causing me to bend at the waist to keep my wrists in their sockets. I'm stretched, and I know when I feel his hands on my back, that I'm in for it right now.

A featherlight touch scorches its way down my spine until he reaches my panties. With a swift tug, they're at my thighs. I'm about to glance over my shoulder, but the heat of his breath at my core is enough to have me trembling.

"What are you—"

The words are broken when his mouth finds purchase on my pussy. His tongue dips into me, delving into the heat of my body, lapping and suckling on me. My legs feel weak, wobbly as he continues to devour me, inch by inch.

A finger trails over the seam of my body, from my throbbing clit to my ass. He teases and taunts, and as I feel the release coiling low in my belly, he stops.

"You're not allowed to come until I'm inside you, sweetheart," he tells me, rising behind me. I half expect him to plunge into me.

I ache for him to, but he doesn't. He saunters away, leaving me trembling and needy.

When he returns moments later, he lifts the whip, crop, or flogger, I can't see, and brings it down on my ass, once, twice, three times and I'm whimpering, wanting more, less, something, anything he has to offer.

He spanks me again. Then once more before he trails his fingers over my body. The gentle touch contrasting with the harsh swats have my core drenched. I can feel the cool breeze of the flogger as he swings it back and forth.

"Are you needy, my pet?" Kian asks in his deep, dominant voice, the sound rumbling from deep in his chest.

"Yes, Master," I whimper, knowing I'm in for more punishment and pleasure. The leather strokes my skin, licking at my flesh as he teases it over the heat between my legs, then, with a soft whoosh, he brings it down over my thighs, my ass. I'm rising up on my tiptoes, and the more he lashes me, the more my pussy drips with arousal.

Suddenly, silence falls around us and I'm breathing heavily. The short quick spurts that fall from my mouth are the only sounds in the room. I don't dare move. I stay as still as possible, waiting.

My body is tingling. It's ready for him to finally fill me. To give me the orgasm and release I've been craving for so long. I'm about to turn my head when the sound of the whip falls onto the smooth wooden floor and then the echoing hiss of a zipper.

I'm hyper aware of him behind me. His heat. His hardness. Everything that Kian is, pure unadulterated male. He oozes sex appeal, confidence, and passion. And when I hear the material of his slacks moving I know I'm about to feel him.

"Are you on the pill, sweetheart?" he questions.

"Yes, Master, and…" I want to tell him, but I don't. I can't find the words.

His hand comes down on my ass harshly. Silence meets me for

a moment before I hear the tearing of foil. "Tomorrow, we'll get tests done." He grits through clenched teeth, and when I glance at him over my shoulder, I watch as he slides the rubber over his thick erection.

"I've not been with anyone since… I mean in years."

"It doesn't matter," he looks up at me, his hand still gripping his cock. "Safety comes first, then we'll play without this," he points to the condom.

"Yes, Master."

With that, he slams into my pussy, bottoming out in one long thrust, and I cry out his name. The sound barrels around us, surrounding us in just that one word, and then he starts moving.

His body slams into mine, fucking me. There's violence in his movements, but there's gentleness in his hold on me. His cock thickens. It pulses as he continues to thrust, filling me like I've never been before.

His thumb finds my tight ring of muscle and swirls it around, taunting me where no man has ever been.

"You're tight, sweetheart," he says with clear awe in his tone.

"Yes, Master," I breathe the words as I tremble beneath him. My arms are tugging painfully, but it's the pleasure that's zipping through me like a live wire, ready to set me alight.

Kian pulls out, all the way, then slams into me once more. His fingers grip my hips so hard he's leaving bruises.

"Come for me, sweetheart," he commands from behind me. Reaching forward, he circles my clit, harder and faster, working me into a frenzy of trembling limbs and unintelligible whimpers and moans. He doesn't relent, making me his plaything until I see stars.

My body shudders as I call out his name again and again.

His shaft throbs inside and I feel his own release follow.

~

WHEN I OPEN MY EYES, I FEEL A HEAVY ARM DRAPED OVER MY WAIST. Kian is behind me, holding me so close I can barely breathe, but I don't move. Waking him is the last thing I want to do so I lie there, staring at the closed blinds, I smile to myself. Last night was something else, and the fact that he's still here is a miracle.

At least, that's how it feels.

His warmth cocoons me, keeping me safe in the memory of how he felt inside me. How he makes me feel like I'm normal for wanting what I do.

I'm not sure what I expected when I woke up this morning in his bed, but this wasn't it. Perhaps it's because he left me alone in mine the last time we were together. The rise and fall of his chest causes his skin to touch mine, making me shiver with need which coils deep in my gut. The desire that he elicits from me is new, and I want more. It's as if I'm hungry and I can't be sated.

"Are you going to lie there all morning and not breathe?" Kian's deep lilt comes from behind me, his hot breath feathering over my ear. He turns me molten with every word, and each touch.

"I figured once I'd passed out you would've woken up and saved me," I smile, turning over under the heavy weight of his arm. Those deep brown eyes that look right through me and see the darkest parts of me glitter with mischief.

"If you sass me I'll spank you."

"If you spank me I might like it." This time I do earn myself a swat on the ass causing me to yelp.

"Don't be a naughty kitten early in the morning," he murmurs, his tone still heavy with sleep which only makes his accent more prominent. That in turn doesn't help my burning need to have him inside me again.

Smiling, I lean forward, planting a kiss on the corner of his mouth and he pulls me in closer, wrapping my body around his as if we can become one person rather than the two broken people we are when we're apart.

The realization courses through me, but I don't say anything. Instead, I bask in his affection when he kisses my cheeks, nose, and forehead before stealing my mouth. A low groan rumbles in his throat and I can feel his erection prodding my stomach.

"I need to get to the office for a meeting, but I want you to stay here. Use my computer to work," he tells me through kisses.

"I have to—"

"Can you log into your email from here?" his voice serious and I nod. "Then you'll stay here. I want you here when I get home. I want to capture you with my camera very soon, my pet." It's a promise. One I'm looking forward to. I've always been shy, but there's something about how he makes me feel that offers me the confidence to nod.

With that, he gives me one final toe-curling kiss and leaves me in bed. I lie there, not wanting to move, but by the time he heads out to work, I know I have to call the office. Grabbing my phone from the bedside table, I hit dial on Gladys' number and press the device to my ear.

"Roisin," she greets, her voice calm. But that's when she's at her most venomous.

"Ms. Caldwell, I've not been feeling very well since last night, so the interview may be slightly delayed. I'm sorry to do this at the last minute. I'm not sure—"

"Roisin," she interrupts me, biting out my name in frustration. "If you can't do this, I'll put someone else on it. You'll be demoted back to the shitty little one-liners for the cover."

My heart sinks at the thought of going back to the job I was doing when I first started. It was soul destroying.

"I trust you'll get this done," she commands.

Nodding, I whisper, "Yes, I told you I can, like I said I've just caught a bug."

"Well un-catch the damn thing and get your interview in. I'm not a complete tyrant, you have forty-eight hours. I trust your *bug* will have gone by then?"

"Yes, yes it will. I—"

The line goes dead before I can say anything more. I've bought myself some time, but I know she's not going to let this go a second time. And that makes more than just my heart sink. I need to figure out how to bring this up to Kian.

KIAN

It's been three days since we've been waking up beside each other. Every morning, I open my eyes to find her beside me and I couldn't be happier. And each night we're in my bed, in my playroom, and I lose myself in her. We've both been for our STI tests, ensuring we're safe, and I look forward to taking her body without anything between us. No more barriers.

She's been working from home, but she hasn't told me what it is that's keeping her busy during the day, and I don't force. I've come to find that Roisin will tell me when she's ready.

I wanted her to confess to me, to tell me about her past, but I couldn't bring myself to ask her again. Each night I'm with her, I find myself not wanting to see sadness in her eyes. But I know she hides so much pain, that all I want to do is save her from it.

I haven't had her pose for me yet. I've waited, given her time to get used to being naked around me. I noticed how she would shy away from me at times, but now it's time to take her to the next level. To see if she's strong enough to handle more.

She moves through the shadow and I watch from my spot in the darkness. Slowly, but surely, as soon as the light illuminates her, my body is alive with want. My blood thrums, humming a melody she's forced upon me. I don't know what's gotten into me. This isn't right. She's too broken. I'll only damage her more, but I can't help myself.

My phone dings with an alert. Her gaze falls on the window, as if she can sense me watching from below. As if she can feel my eyes drinking her in, savoring her drop after drop. Swiping the screen, I tap open the message.

The heartbeat that pulses between my thighs is yours.

The hunger that races through my veins is because of you.

And the way my arousal soaks my fingers is how I want to drench you.

FUCK.

My dick throbs, fighting against the constraints of my slacks. I want to violate her body in the filthiest way. Before I have time to think, my feet move forward. I'm at her door in seconds, pressing the illuminated number.

"Hello?" Her voice is tentative. I can hear the tremble in the word.

"Open this door," I growl into the speaker.

"Kian?"

"It's Master to you, baby girl. Now open the fucking door." My order is harsh, but my mind is awash with filthy images of what I'm about to do to the little tease. She's taunted me, fucked with me using words. Now, I'm going to fuck with her using my fingers, tongue, and cock.

The buzzer sounds and I push the door open, stepping inside. The heat outside is stifling, but the air conditioning inside the foyer cools me somewhat. I make my way to the elevators and up to her floor with my fist gripping my phone tightly.

Her front door beckons me. As if I'm tethered to this fragile, broken girl. I knock twice, sharp, harsh wraps on the wood. When she opens the door, I'm met with fiery red waves, big blue eyes, and her sinful body in a white strapless dress. Her tits are smaller than my hand, but they're pert and jiggle when she moves backward, allowing me entrance into her condo.

"Why did you come here?" she questions, watching me in her home, invading her personal space like I own it. And I want to. So much so that I'm about to break all my fucking rules and regulations.

I shouldn't be getting involved with her. I shouldn't even allow myself to think about her. My job doesn't allow me much personal time. But I don't care. Not when I turn around and glance at her again.

I don't respond to her question with words. Actions speak louder. I close the distance between us, backing her against the door. Her breathing hitches in her throat, her chest rising and falling in huffs. The thin material that covers her braless tits doesn't hide those hardened nipples.

The music filters around us and I hear the chorus of Damien Rice singing *9 Crimes.* The melody is sad, almost melancholy, and I want to leave her, to tell her to get on with her life and forget about me, but I know I'll never be able to forget her.

"You wanted me here," I tell her, allowing my head to drop closer to her face. "Were you on your bed touching your pretty cunt when you sent me that message?" I question, trailing my lips over her cheek. The soft scent of cherries on her skin makes the dominant part of me want to taint her, taste her, watch her shatter for me.

"I was," she confesses. A blush on her cheeks matches the sweet fruit she smells of. Leaning forward even farther, I allow my lips to ghost over her ear. Suckling the fleshy lobe into my mouth, I bite down hard, causing her to yelp.

"You realize that will earn you a punishment," I tell her. "You were touching what's mine."

"Then hurt me." Her plea has a direct link to my cock. It wants her. To fuck her into oblivion, but I rein in my need. Just for a little longer.

"Go to the kitchen, bring me a glass of ice and a wooden spoon."

She spins on her heel and pads into the kitchen. I take in the space that's dimly lit. The shadows it casts over the living room make for a perfect scene. The need to capture her with my lens is something I've been tempted to do, but I don't know if she'll allow me to just yet.

When my little pet returns, she's got a large glass of ice and a wooden spoon that will be a perfect implement to punish her with. My cock agrees when I picture her perfect porcelain skin darkened with red welts.

"What are you going to do?" she asks timidly. The submissive sweetness she exudes only serves to turn me on even more.

"Bend over the arm of the sofa. Hold on to the cushions, because this is going to hurt."

She moves quietly to the black suede sofa and I wonder how many times she's splayed herself on the dark material touching her pretty little cunt. Gracefully, she bends at the waist, the arm of the seat pressing into her stomach. Her hands splay in front of her on the cushions and she grips them with delicate fingers that turn white in a harsh grip.

I know she's scared. She's new to everything I've shown her, and as much as I take my time, there are moments she begs for more. It's in those moments I'd love to really unleash myself on her, but I know I have to take it slow. Her shattered soul is tarnished with what she's endured, and the fear in her gaze when she spoke about her past broke me. What she did to me the first night made me care, and I'm not a man who feels for anyone anymore.

"Do you remember your safe word, pet?"

"Yes, Master. It's yellow to slow down, or red to stop." Her voice is muffled by the seating, but I hear her loud and clear. I think if she was anywhere in the fucking world I'd hear her.

"Good girl," I murmur.

Her slim frame shudders with the two words uttered to her with pride and adoration. I stalk closer to her, taking in the skimpy panties that peek at me from under her white cotton dress. The soft blue material covers what I want to see. It hides what I want to own. And I know there's no longer any way I can walk out of here without claiming my little Rosie.

Lifting the hem of her dress, I bunch it around her hips. With both fingers hooked in the waistband of her panties, I tug them down and find the treasure of her pussy. Her ass, pert, round globes ripe for a spanking. I set the glass on the table and the wooden spoon beside it.

"Did you touch your pretty pussy?" I question while palming the cheeks, squeezing them until she's whimpering into the cushions. "Answer me, pet."

"Yes, Master," comes her muffled response.

"And did you get wet and needy for me?"

"Yes, Master," she says once more, pleasing me with her obedience. I didn't think she'd disobey me, nor did I ever imagine she'd submit to the way I'm manhandling her.

My finger trails over the crack of her ass, her skin erupting in goose bumps as I inch down toward her slick lips. The glistening arousal is enough to drench my finger. I bring it up to my mouth, sucking her juices from my digit.

"And were you going to come without my permission?"

I kneel behind her, running my nose along the smooth skin of her inner thigh, first the left, then the right. Her knees wobble, her moans are soft, but I hear them from where I'm perched behind her.

"Are you going to answer me?" I question, rising and reaching for the spoon. I wait for her response, my hand posed to rain down a harsh spank on her ass.

"I wanted to."

Three little words earns her a blushing red mark on the left creamy cheek of her ass. "And?" I gift her with another, this time on the right. Then the left, then the right. Alternating. The movement makes her feet slip on the wood floor.

"Please," she whimpers, her ass lifting as she rises up onto tiptoes each time.

"What did you want, Rosie?" I continue punishing her for touching my pussy. I fucking own it. Even though she doesn't wear my collar just yet, she will. One day, I'll lay claim to her, but right now she needs to learn every action has a reaction.

"I… I… Fuck me, please, Master?"

That's what I wanted. Those words. That pleading of her needing me the same way I need her.

"Do you want me to fuck your wet pussy? Or are you offering me your tight virgin ass?" I lean in, my mouth at her ear.

She shakes her head, tears streaming down her face. So fucking beautiful. Her ass must be stinging and I know just how I'm going to ease it.

"Tell me!"

"My pussy, please?"

Nodding, I grab the glass, taking one cube of ice and trailing it over her reddened backside. Water trickles down her thighs. I take another block of ice and place it against her pussy. She inhales a sharp breath when I ease the cube into her hole. Slick with arousal, wet with the water, and so warm inside. It melts and runs down her inner thighs, which is what I needed to lean in and lap at her core.

My tongue darts into her cunt, fucking her gently as I grip her ass cheeks, opening her to my tongue. I move higher, finding her taut ring of muscle, which she involuntarily clenches at the contact I make.

"If you clench your ass, I'll fuck it. I don't care if you're a virgin, I'll force my dick so deep inside, you won't be able to sit down for a week." My warning is clear. She obeys, calming herself so I can devour both her tiny holes.

With two fingers, I dip into her pussy while I lick and taunt her ass. The tension is gone when she finally allows me to use her. Crooking my fingers inside her, I stroke the spot that causes her to cry out her release as she comes hard over my hand.

Soon, I'll make her squirt. She'll give me everything she never gave anyone else. I'll have not only her mind, but her body, heart, and her soul. All her pleasure and pain will come from me. I pull her panties up her thighs and make sure they're in place before I continue.

"Stand. Eyes on the floor," I tell her, my voice echoing in the space around us. "You'll suck my cock until I feel you're ready to get fucked."

She rises, instinctively meeting my gaze, then quickly dropping them. I should punish her. I want to. But I won't. Not this time. She's learning. New to my world.

"I want you to kneel on the carpet, then take out my dick and keep your eyes on what you're doing."

"Yes, Master." She drops to her knees, and I miss her eyes on me, but for now, I want her to focus on the task at hand.

Her delicate fingers work my belt, jeans, and she tugs them down along with the black boxers I'm wearing. My cock, thick and angry, juts out toward her. The small pink tongue darts out and wets her lips. Then she's wrapping those plump lips around the shaft, taking me into her warm mouth inch my inch.

The torture is painful. She moves so slow. My hand fists her long hair, gripping it harshly.

"I said suck it," I bite out. Her hands fall to her sides. Then, she shocks me speechless when she places both hands behind her back in a show of submission that even my ex-wife couldn't give me until our second month together.

My hips move of their own volition. I pull out, until the tip is on her tongue, then slam into her tight throat, causing her to gag loudly. Spit drips from her chin onto her virginal dress. I should've taken it off. Seeing her small tits coated in her saliva would've set me off, so I close my eyes and breathe deeply while I continue to fuck her mouth.

Her nose hits my groin time and again. I move faster, losing myself in the control. The violent need that races through my veins hums with pleasure as my heart beats for my little Rosie. A flower. An innocent, sweet girl.

My submissive.

My slave.

My pet.

Pulling out of her mouth, I release her. With one step back, I take her in. Tears have streaked her face. The front of her dress is drenched. She's watching me with big blue eyes that are crystal clear, even though she'd just been crying.

I only know this because her nose and cheeks are bright red.

"I'm… Shit… I didn't…"

"Thank you, Master," she utters, not cleaning herself, just kneeling, sitting on her heels as she smiles at me. Her hands remain behind her back.

"I hurt you."

"I need you to hurt me," she confesses with a pained response.

Shaking my head, I glance at my painfully hard cock.

"Would you like me to continue?" Her question jars me. She really fucking wants this?

"How does an innocent girl like you want this life?" This time, it's my turn to cause her to sit back and think about my words.

"I do this to myself." Slowly, ever so slowly, she lifts the hem of her dress to show me her upper thighs and then, she pulls the item up and over her head and there, on her flat, smooth stomach are the silvery scars that almost make me sick. "I need the pain to feel. To stop the anxiety. When I bleed, the images in my head don't haunt me."

I close the distance I put between us, cupping her face in my hands. For a moment, we watch each other. Just with the sound of our breathing. Sweet, serene, wanting.

"I want to help you," I utter, my eyes boring into hers. It's my confession. I want her to feel everything she's meant to. Happiness, pleasure, joy, love.

The last word stills me.

Do I want her to love me?

No.

All I want is for her to know there's pleasure out there. Perhaps I can teach her. But then again, I only know how to show pleasure through pain.

Am I really good for her?

"Don't overthink this," she breathes. The sparkling blue of her irises shine in the soft glow of her lamp. Dark lashes and eye liner make them pop from her porcelain skin. She looks like a toy. A doll. And oh, how I want to play with her.

"This is not easy, Rosie," I confide. "There are things in this lifestyle that are dark, sometimes dangerous."

"I've seen far worse in my life. Nothing you can do will scare me."

"I'll never scare you. If you want this, me, I'll give it to you. I'll show you this life, this world of pleasure and pain, but I want you to promise me something, my sweet Rosie."

ROISIN

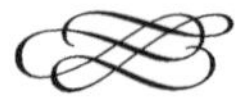

I watch him for a moment before nodding.

"Anything." I don't know how much I believe the word I utter, but I say it anyway. If this is a way out of the hell I've been living, I'll take it. I'll take anything he offers because even though I don't know much about Kian, I know he won't be violent or do the things I've seen in foster care.

My first foster father was a pastor, but he was worse than Satan. The Bible was what he hid behind when he took me and my two foster sisters to church to pray.

"You need to be honest. This will not work if you can't tell me something. As a Master, I want to own everything about you, but first, I need you to give me every part of you. I will never force you, push you beyond what you can take. Between us, there can be no secrets, no fear. This is a test of trust. Ultimate, unconditional trust."

Nodding, I sigh, rising to my feet when he offers me both his hands. His cock is still hard between us as he pulls me into an embrace that steals my breath and I fear that if he continues showing me this affection, he'll steal my soul too.

My childhood was filled with lies, violence, and abuse. And

when gentle caring is given, I lap it up like a hungry kitten. Ravenous for the touches, the calming words, and the way he holds me so close I feel safer than I have in years.

"Kian." I step back, meeting his inquisitive gaze, which in this low light is dark, almost black. But I know that in the sunshine, his eyes are the color of warm chocolate. "I can't give you everything all in one sitting, but…"

My words taper off.

The thud of my heart is deafening. I can't hear myself think.

He takes my hands, brings them up to his mouth, and plants kisses on my knuckles. "In a few moments, I'll have you lying on the bed where I'll take you slowly, like I admire every inch of you. It will be gentle. I'll claim you sweetly, and ever so lovingly, but tomorrow, when we wake up, I'm going to fuck you so hard, so violently, and I'll make you scream."

He follows me toward my bedroom. The blue curtains hang across the large windows, shielding us from sight as we enter the space I've never allowed anyone else inside. Not even my best friend has been inside my room. It's always been *my* space.

"Your room is perfectly you," he murmurs behind me, his hands on my hips, holding me against his erection that fits between my ass cheeks.

"Thank you, Master." My words are a breathy whisper, tentative but needy.

He trails his fingers over my exposed flesh. "Take off this dress and get on the bed. Leave your panties on." His order is dark, a low husky rumble that seems to vibrate through me.

I move without flinching. Without thinking. I want him so much. I reach for the hem of my dress, pulling it up and over my head. The cool air races over my body, causing my bare nipples to harden.

Dropping the material on the floor, I climb onto the bed, rolling over onto my back. The evening is lit by only the silver moon which shines through the tiny slats of the blinds. Kian's bathed in darkness. The shirt he's wearing, the only light color around us, like a beacon in the night.

He's mine.

The thought drifts through my mind unbidden, but when I try to push it away, it settles there like a lead weight. Kian stalks closer, unbuttoning his crisp white shirt with his dark brown eyes pinned on me.

"You're perfect," he murmurs as his shirt finds a spot beside my dress.

My eyes drink him in. Even without the brightness of the overhead bulb I can make out his taut muscles that are clear when he leans in closer to me. There's a gentle definition to his abs, his arms. Everything about him is manly.

A light dusting of hair on his chest makes me want to feel him against me. He doesn't say a word as he moves lower, toward my stomach. And when he plants soft kisses on my scars, tears burn my eyes.

The moment is sweet, almost loving as he traces the silvery lines with his fingers, then his lips. I watch in awe as a man who's worth more than a broken girl who's been unwanted all her life shows me affection that's never before been gifted to me.

When his eyes meet mine once more, he smiles. "These make you more beautiful. The scars you bear are the proof that you're strong. That you're not some broken little girl, but you're a strong woman who can do anything. And that," he says with conviction, "makes you sexy." With that, he dips between my legs, spreading my thighs and inhaling me as if I were the most decadent dessert.

His fingers tug at my panties, pulling the material down my thighs and dropping them on the floor. When he turns his attention back to me, the look he offers is feral, hungry, and filled with need. "Open your legs," he growls. I do. They splay as wide as I can manage and that's when he rains down a swat on my slick pussy.

"Oh!" I cry out, the sensation tingling through my body,

rippling over my skin like an electric current trailing its way over me.

"Don't." Slap.

"Touch." Slap.

"What's mine." Slap.

My body shudders wildly. My hands fist the sheets in a white-knuckle grip when he continues his harsh punishment. And I know deep down, this is just want I need. He knows what I want. My thighs tremble, my nipples are hard peaks, and when he reaches up to tweak one, I can't take anymore and my release races through me.

My arousal soaks the bed below me. It trickles between my ass cheeks. I open my eyes to find Kian staring at me with wonderment and satisfaction on his handsome face.

"Do you understand?" he questions. I nod. "And next time you have an orgasm without my permission, you won't be able to sit down for a week." The corner of his mouth kicks up in a smirk that's pure sin. He shoves his slacks down, the thick erection juts out from between his legs, and I can't help licking my lips.

"Can I... I mean..."

"No, tonight is for you," he tells me, nestling between my thighs. His hips fit perfectly against me and the tip of his cock presses against my pussy. "You remember your pill, baby girl?"

"Yes," I whisper, my cheeks reddening. No man I've ever had near me has asked me outright if I've taken my pill, or even cared about my well-being. Most of them were only concerned with their pleasure. The thought brings back a memory I'd rather not recall.

"Look into my eyes," Kian orders, causing my gaze to snap up to his. Ever so slowly, he pushes inside me, my body tightening around his cock as it invades my pussy. He's thick, hard, and warm. With every inch he enters me with, I whimper and moan. The illicit sounds of sex echo around us like a symphony of pleasure and happiness.

My back arches when he finally seats himself fully inside me. "Kian," I moan out his name as the crown of his cock hits a spot inside me that causes me to see stars behind my closed eyelids. He doesn't ask me to look at him again. Instead, he continues to move. Pulling out and inching back in.

Our bodies move. Back and forth. Up and down. "That's my girl," he praises me with admiration. "You're beautiful, Rosie," he tells me, his accent inkling toward the Scottish lilt. The sound is a rumble. Decadent and delicious, but then he leans in closer, brushing his lips over mine in a teasing kiss. "You may have been broken in the past, but you're no longer *that* girl," he tells me.

My eyes open, widen at the emotion dancing in his deep brown eyes that remind me of warmth and safety. It darkens depending on his mood, from a milk chocolate to a decadent dark cocoa.

I can't answer him, because when I open my mouth, words evade me. That's when he sees the tears. My eyes well up, and he moves. Faster, harder, deeper. He pistons into me.

"If you want to hurt," he tells me on a thrust. "I'll fucking hurt you," once again, his words vibrate through his chest and into mine. Wild and unrestrained.

My toes curl with every drive. My nails find purchase in the skin of his shoulders, trying to ground myself. To find some sort of root, because I'm about to be cast off a cliff.

Kian's mouth suckles my exposed neck, biting down on the skin. I know he's bruising me. He continues to devour me as if he's trying to mark me as his. My thighs tremble. My hard nipples brush against his chest.

Our bodies are slick with sweat. Heat. Desire. Rage. There's anger in the way he moves. His hips now slam into me. Pressing me into the mattress, he continues to own me. To claim me. I know that's what he's doing because I feel it right down to my core.

"Come for me, pet," he utters in my ear, then his teeth break the sensitive flesh on my nape, which causes my nails to dig in farther tearing at his shoulders, and down his back. I cry out as I crest. A wave crashing on the shore. I was lost, broken, and shattered for so long, that Kian somehow knows I need the pain to feel alive. And he gives it to me with pleasure rather than vengeance.

His body locks as he empties himself inside me. Filling me up to the brink, he lifts his head, eyes sparkling like gemstones.

"You're okay?" This time, he looks more concerned about me than when he was punishing me moments ago.

"I haven't been better."

My words ease the frown between his dark brows. I wince when he slips from my body. He turns, leaving me on the bed, a spent mess. When he returns to the room, he's carrying a cloth. Gently, he cleans me and settles on the bed, pulling me into his arms.

"If you ever so much as pick up a sharp object to harm yourself, I'll spank your ass so raw the skin will take weeks to heal." It's a vicious threat, but he coos it like a sweet promise.

"Yes, Master," I purr, curling into him, reveling in his warmth. His large calloused hands stroke my bare flesh, calming my racing heart. My lashes flutter closed and sleep steals me.

JOLTING UP IN BED, I GLANCE OVER MY SHOULDER TO FIND THE BED empty. Sadness washes over me, gripping my heart painfully. My body aches when I roll onto my back. The ceiling is bathed in the orange hues of an early morning.

I have to get my article in today, but I didn't get a chance to ask Kian if it would be okay to write about him. I should've brought it up, but I didn't want to anger him and risk him walking out. I've already delayed it, and I know if I do so once more, I'll get written up and demoted.

I should message him, ask him if I could perhaps write an anonymous recollection, but this isn't something that could be said in a text message. No, this is something I need to talk to him about face-to-face.

A memory from last night lingers, Kian inside me. His body moving with mine. Last night I was more than a broken girl, I was a woman desired by a man.

A man who's now left me. Walked out before I even opened my eyes. Sighing, I push off the bed, the soft ache between my legs a reminder of what we did. I wrap myself in my robe and make my way to the kitchen.

Once the coffee pot is brewing, I pad over to my desk, turning on my MacBook. I might as well work. Get lost in words rather than images that play on a loop in my mind. As much as I want Kian, perhaps it's better that he wasn't here when I woke up.

I wanted him to care. I wanted to finally find something more than just a one-night stand and I believed him, but I don't know anything about him. I'm lost in thoughts when my phone buzzes on the cabinet.

The screen lights up, and from where I'm standing, I can see his name. My fingers itch to touch it, to touch him, but I don't move. Instead, I watch the screen go dark. A niggle in my chest, one I've never felt sparks to life.

When it lights up again, I pick it up. A voicemail. Hitting dial, I put it on speaker and settle on my chair.

"Pet, I had to get to work. I didn't want to leave you this morning, but you looked so peaceful, I left you to sleep. Don't you dare doubt me. I'll call you later."

Click.

My heart thuds wildly at his promise. *Call you later.* Once again, I'm hanging onto his every word. It's happened before. My young, broken heart still beats, still craves attention. Leaving my phone on the desk, I head back into the kitchen.

My skin prickles in awareness as I pour my coffee. The sunlight glows through the window, golden light warming the black marble countertop. The last time I'd truly enjoyed the sun was when I finally ran from my foster parents. When I walked out of the home I'd known for two years of my life.

An eighteen-year-old girl.

My childhood memories will always be tainted. Since before I was taken in by the Pastor and his wife took me in, to the moment I came of age. I've pushed away the images in my mind, but now and again, I get glimpses of them. Lifting the mug to my lips, I take a long sip. The hot liquid burns its way down my throat.

Each night I've spent with Kian has offered me a sense of normalcy. He's made me feel like I'm wanted. He's offered me a choice to experience his world. Not forced to do things I didn't want to. I should tell Kian about my past, about the things that've happened to me, but I know as soon as he finds out just how broken I am, he'll turn and walk away.

But then again, he knows I have a past that's dark and sordid. He may believe he knows how to fix me, and maybe, with his way of affection he's offered me solace, but I doubt I can ever be truly whole. But the truth is mine to keep. As long as he doesn't find out, we can make this work.

Sighing, I fill my mug once more and head to my desk to start work. I settle on the chair, opening my email, and see my next brief is ready and waiting for me. Scrolling through the emails, I glance at the subject lines. One in particular jumps out at me.

Another invitation to Runway. At first, I think it's Greer, she loves clubbing, parties, but when I click on the link and scan the email, I know it's not her.

Friday night.

Nine in the evening.

A dinner and scene in one of the rooms with an unnamed host.

I know who it is the moment my gaze lands on those two words. *Unnamed host.* It can't be anyone other than Kian.

He didn't mention it.

He didn't even ask if I'd ever like to go back to Black Light. Closing the email, I focus on work and push the invite to the back of my mind.

KIAN

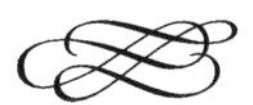

"Kian." Mikael saunters into my office with a grin. "I found our blonde babydoll," he tells me with a shit-eating grin. "She was holed up in Beverly Hills. One of our informants picked her up two hours ago."

"Good." I turn my attention back to my computer. The information I found on Roisin has all my attention and I can feel my partner's questioning gaze burning through me. "It's Rosie."

"Shit, dude, you really like this one." His observation isn't far off. I do like her, so much so that I went out this morning to purchase a collar.

"She's different, nothing like any woman I've been with in the past, and I'm planning on making her mine," I tell him, leaning back in my office chair. I've never seen my friend so shocked before. His mouth is agape as he stares at me.

"You're serious?"

I've thought about it over the past week. Being around her is like a breath of fresh air. Teaching her, guiding her. There's nothing more satisfying than letting her experience the pleasure of my lifestyle and watching her take to it like she's been born to do it.

"Listen, Kian, I know she's beautiful and you love her innocence, but..." His words taper off and I know what he's thinking. Her past is dotted with darkness. That's something she and I still need to talk about. I want her to trust me, but I also need her to open up on her own. I can't force her to.

"I know she has darkness in her past, but I have to wait until she comes to me," I tell him.

He nods because he knows I'm right. I may not know everything she's been through, but what I do know is that she's mine. I'm not letting her go.

"As long as you know what you're getting yourself into," he offers, settling in the chair opposite from me. "I have a meeting with a new client later."

"Oh?"

"Yeah, some asshole looking for his estranged wife." Mikael chuckles. He's always found it funny when wives go missing, but I didn't, mainly because Siobhan left without a forwarding address. Just a note to say goodbye and I was alone. There was nothing more for me in our home, so I sold it and moved.

When I arrived in Los Angeles, I knew I needed to put down roots, the only reason being that I never wanted to feel like a stranger in my home again. When I bought the mansion, it was mine. No other woman who walked in there had embedded herself in the space. No woman, until Roisin.

"Good luck, I've got to plan how I'm going to present this damn collar to her," I tell him, watching his eyebrows shoot up in shock. I told him not so long ago that I'd consider it, but only if I found the right woman. I didn't plan on finding someone who captured me so much though. It's always been a second thought when I'm with a submissive, but with my red-haired vixen I've become the needy one. Rosie has certainly given me something I can no longer deny. She's made me feel.

"This is a turn of events," he says, watching me.

Nodding, I lean back in my chair, meeting his inquisitive gaze.

"It is," I agree easily. I could never lie to my best friend. He'll see right through me if I act nonchalant about this.

"And you think she'll agree? To a collar?"

"Yes." I've never been more sure about anything in my life.

He sighs, and I wonder if he's thinking about ever taking on a full-time submissive. The reason Mikael and I get along so well is because we're one and the same. We enjoy playing the field.

"Good luck, Kian," he tells me then. "I thought you'd never commit, but if she's the one, then go for it. Just make sure you know what you're getting yourself into."

"I will."

He grins. Rising from the seat, he heads for the doorway. "Oh, and one more thing, if she has a friend, hook me up." This time, he chuckles wolfishly as he exits my office, leaving me to wonder what she's doing right this minute. I pull out my phone and send her a message asking her for a photo. Something sweet, innocent.

I don't wait long for a response, because it comes moments later. Roisin sitting at her desk, dressed in a yellow sundress, her long hair loose over her shoulders, and a smile on her face that lights up my entire day.

Good girl.

I HIT SEND AND ATTEMPT TO CONTINUE WORKING, WITHOUT BEING distracted about where tonight will lead us.

AS SOON AS I WALK INTO THE HOUSE, I HEAD STRAIGHT FOR THE room where I've photographed countless women. But tonight, I'll be with Rosie. I'll see her at her most vulnerable. There's something about being behind the lens. It offers you a glimpse into someone's soul.

Although, I've already seen her, seen deep into the parts she keeps hidden. I've waited, but tonight, I want her to tell me everything. And I know exactly how I'm going to have her confess.

I turn on the lights as I go, illuminating the space as I head straight for the playroom. Inside, I pull out the implements I want to use for our scene. Giving her time to adjust to everything has been difficult because all I want to do is mark her. Tonight, we'll play with her senses. I'll blindfold her, bind her, and have her completely at my mercy.

I pick up the three large lavender candles, lighting them as I place them on the wooden shelf against one wall. The room is comfortably warm, which is perfect since I'll be photographing her naked. I can't wait to see her pose, having the flames cast shadows on her perfect skin, over the slight curves of her body.

The doorbell rings promptly at seven p.m. and I can't help smiling at how punctual she is. It's one of my pet peeves—tardiness. Soon she'll have her own key, but for now, I'll let her in. I saunter to the front door and pull it open.

My breath is knocked from my lungs at the vision before me. She's plaited her long hair, tying it behind her. Her body is encased in a silky red dress that offers a hint at the curves of her breasts. The hemline stops short of her cunt, giving me a view of her lithe legs. Her feet are perched in four-inch stilettos that match the fire engine down the road.

"Well, pet." I admire her. "Don't you look ready to be ravished," I tell her, offering her my hand. When she slips her dainty hand in mine, I lead her inside, shutting the door behind us.

"Thank you, Sir." She smiles, blushing lightly at the way my gaze roams over her body.

"I trust no other man has seen you in this," I ask, tugging at the cowl-neck, allowing me to glimpse her tits, nipples hardening as I stare at them.

"No, Sir, I came straight here. Nobody else has seen me."

I nod with a smile. That's what I wanted to hear. I'm far too obsessed with this woman, but nothing is going to stop me now.

I lead her down the hallway, toward the room where I'm going to photograph her, but also learn more about her.

"Tonight, I want to take a few photos," I tell her as we stroll farther down the hallway. "Would you be okay with that?" I glance at her, waiting for her to refuse, to perhaps tell me it's too much, but she doesn't.

"I'd like that." She nods and smiles. "Are we eating first?"

Smiling, I nod when I feel her eyes on me. Her curiosity has always made me smile.

"Yes, sweetheart." I open the door, ushering her inside.

A soft gasp falls from her lips when she finds the table set up in the playroom. I wanted to eat in the room where we've played our scenes so she's comfortable in the space for the shoot later. I've noticed her nervous energy each time we've come in here, and I know she's waiting for me to ask about her past again.

"Sit," I order, pulling out the chair for her.

Once she's comfortable, I make my way around the table, gesturing for her to lift the silver dome covering her plate. When she does, she smiles.

"Did you make this?" Her mouth tilts into a shy smile.

"No, sweetheart, I had my maid make dinner. I hardly ever make my way into the kitchen and I've been at work all day," I tell her. As soon as I walked into the kitchen earlier, I knew Mishka had finished the dinner I requested.

"It smells good," she tells me.

Taking the fork, she scoops a mouthful onto the utensil. I watch in awe of her beauty as she eats her food. I can't tear my gaze away from her to eat my own, but I don't need to. I want to make sure she's got a good meal before we play tonight.

"Are you going to watch me all night?" Rosie quips.

"I can't help it if my muse is far too distracting for me to concentrate on anything else," I tell her, taking my first bite of the steak and salad that's been sitting on my plate untouched.

"Fair enough." She shrugs. Her shoulders lift and fall easily. Roisin sits back, her eyes never leaving mine as she lifts her water glass, bringing it to her full lips. She sips the drink, but her eyes are on me, fire flirting through them as she stares at me.

"Take your dress off, sweetheart," I command, gesturing with my finger for her to rise.

She stands, slipping the slinky material from her shoulders. The dress falls, pooling at her heeled feet. Her eyes remain focused on the floor. The smooth skin that I'm met with makes me groan.

"Step out of the dress, bend over the center of the table like a good girl, because I'm dying to fuck you like a bad one," I tell her.

Silently, she moves, leaving the garment on the floor and she positions herself bent at the waist in the middle of the table between my plate and hers. I lift my Merlot and stand, stalking behind her. I lean in and plant soft kisses down her spine. A gentle shiver travels over her body.

I kick her feet apart, her hands gripping the opposite edge of the wooden table. Swiftly, I rain down two harsh swats on her pert ass cheeks, watching them turn a soft shade of blush.

"Count for me, gorgeous," I command her, swatting her again.

"One," she whispers.

Swat.

"Two."

Swat.

"Three."

Swat.

"Four."

"Good girl," I coo, kissing the reddened flesh with gentle pecks. I kneel behind her then, getting a view of her glistening cunt. The lips are smooth, inviting, and they're needy for me. I lift my wine glass, lean in, and tip liquid down the crack of her beautiful ass. My tongue darts out, catching the trickles causing her to moan loudly. Watching as the liquid trickles over her folds turns me rabid and I'm dying to make her scream.

Once the glass is on the table again, I lean in and lap at her, licking from the mound of her pussy to the small tight ring of her ass. Again and again.

"Now this is what I call a good dinner," I tell her. Opening the cheeks of her ass, I devour her, reveling in the delicious taste of her arousal. It drips steadily on my tongue as I dart it into her body. The heat of Roisin is intoxicating, causing my cock to throb in my slacks. Soft mewls fall from her lips and her knees wobble, but I hold her up, keeping her open for my mouth to feast on.

"Please, Master," she whimpers, "fuck me." Her pleas make me smile against her drenched core.

Releasing her, I rise, slowly unzipping my pants. Once they're shoved to my thighs along with my boxer briefs, I fist my cock, trailing the tip over her pussy, mixing her glistening juices with my own arousal. Once the crown is shiny, I slip into her, inch by inch. I move slowly, taunting her.

Her head moves, her eyes meeting mine over her shoulder. "Please," she begs once more and I can't take it anymore. My hips slam against her ass harshly, pushing her into the edge of the table. Our glasses fly from the surface, crashing to the floor below, but in this moment, I don't care. Moving back, I thrust into her again, fully seating myself in the most beautifully tight cunt I've ever had the pleasure of fucking.

With one hand, I fist her hair, tugging her back. My other hand grips her throat, tightening my hold just enough to have her gasp and her slick walls clench around my cock, sucking me in deeper.

"You like that, pet?" I hiss in her ear, moving almost violently as I fuck her into the hard surface. Her back arches beautifully and her head comes close to my lips as they whisper over her ear. "Do you? You like me using you like my fuck toy?" I bite out, pleasure zipping through me like an electric current that's about to explode all over the goddamn room.

"Yes, yes," she mewls loudly.

"Who owns you, Roisin?" I question, not stopping my assault on her body.

"You, Master. I'm yours." She utters the words I've been dying to hear for days.

With my free hand, I slowly circle her ass, allowing my thumb to slip into the tight hole. Imagining my cock inside her ass only makes me groan louder. Working her pulsing little ring of muscle, I gently scissor her open, watching in awe as she takes two digits inside her. The sight is enough to have me filling her with my seed.

"Good girl," I coo, thrusting at her wet cunt. "Are you ready for this?" I question through clenched teeth as I finger her ass faster, opening her up ensuring she's prepared. I pull out slowly, waiting for her to offer me the confirmation of what I already know. Gripping my now slippery shaft, I position the tip at her ass, nudging into her tight ring of muscle.

"Yes, please, fuck my ass." She nods as much as she can with my hold still on her Rapunzel-like red hair.

My hips buck, causing the tip of my dick to spear her open, eliciting a cry from her plump lips. I wait, holding all my movement. Once she's breathing calmly, I inch into her, almost losing myself in her tightness.

Shutting my eyes, I breathe deeply, attempting to hold off the orgasm that's threatening to overwhelm me. Her body is hot, shuddering beneath me, making me want to violate her beautiful hole until she's a limp mess beneath me.

"Move, Kian, please," she says, snapping me out of the reverie I was in. "Master, I mean Master." Her correction comes too late, because I grit my teeth and shove into her, balls deep inside her tight asshole.

"Fuck, pet," I grunt, feeling my balls draw up, ready to empty into her channel. When I shift, she pulses around me, attempting to milk the seed from me. "If you keep that up, I'll fill this pretty ass with my cum. Is that what you want?" I tug her head back. She's curved so erotically I'm half tempted to take a photo just to jerk off to it later.

"I need you, I want you. Own me." Her words send me soaring higher than any drug could and I no longer hold onto the thin thread of restraint. Instead, I release her hair. Gripping her hips, I pull out, then slam back in, again and again.

I reach around her, circling her clit while I own her little ass. Her cries are otherworldly, and I'm beyond thinking about anything other than my orgasm that's about to rocket through me. When Rosie squeals out, her body squirting juices all over my slacks, I grunt my release into her, filling her, marking her from the inside.

And there's one thing I'm certain of.

She's mine.

ROISIN

I find myself in a dimly lit room that's breathtaking. There's a calmness that overcomes me. It makes me feel ready for what's to come. There are three large candles that bounce shadows from the walls. It's smaller, hidden behind the door in the black room where all his toys are. The floor is a laminate wood that feels smooth under my bare feet.

After we fucked, Kian carried me to the shower, washing me from head to toe. He massaged me because I ached everywhere from the rough handling, but I'd never felt so safe, so loved before. I asked him to own me, and he hadn't sent me packing. I don't want to read too much into it, but something tells me he wants that too.

"I want you on the floor. Kneeling, sitting your pretty ass on your heels, spread your legs, and place your hands on your thighs." His voice is gruff, heavy with need still on every word he utters.

I nod, obeying him without response. I settle myself on the floor. The cool hardwood makes me shiver. My nipples harden from the cold, but I think it's more for Kian than anything else. I place my hands palms up on my thighs as he spoke about earlier. My eyes are on the floor in front of me.

He crouches in front of me, tugging my long hair and positioning it over my shoulders, covering my breasts to his gaze.

"Tonight, I'll capture you with my lens, sweetheart," he tells me. "But everything that belongs to me, your tits, your cunt, will not be visible. These are artistic shots, and I'm the only man who's allowed to see you completely."

"Yes, Master."

He rises once more. His socked feet move across the room as he sets up the camera. The tripod in one corner gets shifted and I can't stop the tremble that moves through me.

"Tell me, sweetheart," he says, then I hear a click. Once with a flash, then another time without the bright light. "Tell me about you, your past."

He takes another shot, moving around me. When he's satisfied with the photos, he moves me to where he wants me. Into poses and, as promised, my body is bare, but covered.

"I was young, living with a foster family. A pastor and his wife," I tell him, finally confessing who I am. "I grew up with God, going to church." The click of the camera doesn't make me shiver anymore. Instead, it offers me solace.

I'm hidden, but opening myself up more than I've ever been, and through the lens I know Kian can see my fear and pain. He can see everything I've hidden through the small viewfinder he looks through. Once he takes a photo, he glances at the tiny screen on the back of the camera, no doubt making sure he's happy with the shot.

"And you no longer go to church." It's not a question, an observation. He must know what happened. Surely he can figure it out. But I know why he's doing this. He wants me to relive it so I can put the past behind me.

I wish I could say goodbye to that life, to who I was. But I can't. Not yet. I'm still that scared little girl. The one who was shunned because of what I wanted, what I needed.

"Tell me, Rosie."

"One day, I was caught with… I had my own room," I tell him as he takes photos. As if he's filming me in still shots, wanting to find the shattered girl beneath my shy exterior. "Father Paulson…" I sigh, not wanting to recall the horror on his face, on his wife's face. "His wife came home early one afternoon while I was doing homework."

It's silent for a moment, no click of the camera to break the tension in the room. I glance up, looking at Kian as he stands behind the tripod, the camera pointed right at me.

"I was writing poems," I tell him. "They were darker, more… illicit."

Kian nods, waiting for the rest.

"She found them on my computer, but it was the images."

"What images, Roisin?"

"I was researching for a project when I found this website," I tell him. My cheeks are burning in the dark and I'm glad he can't see me properly. I remember how ashamed I felt. How embarrassing it was to be caught. "The women were bound." The words spill from my lips, my voice a low whisper. "Naked and bound."

"They were BDSM images," he fills in and I nod. "And you liked them?" This time he does question. I can hear the interest in his voice.

"I'd overheard girls at school talking about things I'd been taught were evil," I whisper. "About touching themselves while looking at pictures. I tried it one night and after growing up in a strict home, I felt guilty after, but each night, I did it again and again."

"It wasn't wrong, Rosie. You were a growing girl with hormones. It was natural for you to be curious, to want to experience something so normal for a teenager." Kian sounds incredibly angry, which causes me to lift my gaze to his.

"I know." I nod. "Well, I know it now. But, she found the photos on the computer," I continue, my fingers knotting within each other as my nerves get the better of me. "She was so angry." I blink, allowing a stray tear to slip from my eye, trickling down my cheek.

"What happened next?"

I shift, sitting my ass on the cool floor, my legs curled under me. Kian doesn't stop taking photos with each movement I make, as if he's attempting to capture every second of me. Of this strange scene.

"He came home, Father Paulson. She told him, showed him." I snap my eyes closed, recalling the moment I'd felt the most excruciating pain I'd ever experienced. "He pulled his thick leather belt out, and..." My voice is a mere whisper and I wonder if Kian can hear me. He doesn't move this time. The click of the shutter doesn't sound and I know he's probably attempting to hear my whispered confession.

"Rosie—"

"He whipped me until I was bleeding. I felt the hot liquid trickle down my body." I choke back a sob, the pain almost real as I talk about it. A melody comes from the surrounding speaker system and I recognize Tom Odell singing *Heal.*

I snap my gaze to Kian, who's no longer at his camera. This time he's standing before me, as if ready to kill my monsters. As if he's trying to keep me safe as he stands at the ready to take down anything wanting to hurt me.

"That night he told me, taught me rather, how girls like me are cured by their devil ways. He became obsessed with curing me, so every night…" I allow the words to trickle to nothing and Kian is on the floor seconds later. His arms around my slight frame as I shake in his hold. The warmth of his touch does nothing to calm me. It does nothing to keep my mind from going back there.

"I'm so sorry," Kian murmurs. "I didn't realize. I mean… I didn't think it would hurt you so much," he tells me, his mouth pressing a kiss to the top of my head. The music, his arms, the lyrics, wash over me in the dark room and I know even though there are times I still feel guilty for enjoying pleasure, I know it's not wrong.

"I never wanted to tell you because I didn't want you to look at me differently."

This time Kian pushes away from me. His eyes bore into me as if I've lost my mind. "Rosie, I could never look at you any other way than I am right now. This"—he gestures between us—"is the most important thing in my life. You are the most important person in my life." His declaration makes my heart thud wildly in my chest. "But what I don't understand is how can you want this life after what you'd been through?"

I have to think about a response to his question because I honestly don't know the answer. Even though my awakening was crude, violent, and forced, I still for some strange reason longed to find a man who could teach me the right way. At times, I do still feel the pain, feel the fear I did each night, but I know somehow, I have to force myself to move on.

"You make things different," I tell him then, reaching for his cheek. I cup it in my hand. "There's something I feel when I'm with you that makes things feel right, like I'm meant to experience pleasure, and it's not a dirty thing I need to be *cured* from."

"Oh, sweetheart," he says, pulling me into his lap and I curl myself there, wanting to never move.

We sit like that for so long, I allow myself to stop crying finally. I breathe in Kian's scent, my eyes flutter closed, and sleep steals me.

~

WHEN I ROLL OVER, MY BODY COCOONED IN HEAVY EGYPTIAN

cotton sheets, I curl into the soft material, cracking one eye to see the sun streaming through the curtains. There's a sliver allowing the light in and I can't help groaning at the thought of getting out of bed.

Straightening my legs, I allow the tension to evaporate when I remember last night, confessing everything to Kian and him not running away. Instead, he held me in his arms until I fell asleep. He must've carried me to bed, because I'm safely in his large king-sized four-poster bed.

It's Friday today, which means I have to work, which is something I'm not looking forward to. I can easily hide in bed forever.

"Good morning, sweetheart." Kian's voice comes from the doorway where he's leaning against the doorjamb. Already dressed in a pair of ironed black slacks, a midnight blue pinstripe shirt with a silver tie, he looks like he's about to head into court, rather than to the office.

"You're up early," I tell him, scooting up, leaning my back against the headboard.

He saunters into the room with a smile on his face and even in the low light, he looks ever the commanding Dominant. The bed dips when he settles beside me, his hand on mine, as he pulls it up to plant a soft kiss on my knuckles.

"I wanted to make you breakfast," he says. "So you better get your sexy little ass out of my bed and come to the kitchen."

"I thought you didn't cook?" I sass him, earning me a low rumbling chuckle.

"I don't. You make me do things I never did before, sweetheart," he offers, but there's something so serious in his gaze that I wonder if we're still talking about cooking.

"And you make me want things I've never wanted before."

He nods as if he knew that already. As if he'd already figured out that my feelings for him are growing stronger by the day. With each moment I spend beside him, I find myself not wanting to leave. And that in itself scares me more than anything ever has.

"I wanted to give something to you last night," Kian says with his gaze on our interlocked fingers, snapping me out of my darkening thoughts. "It's something I bought, in the hope you'd accept me in your life. Not just as someone who will teach you then walk out."

He lifts those dark eyes, meeting mine.

"I want to own you, sweetheart," he rasps. "I want everything you have to give and then so much more." He reaches for the bedside table, opening the small drawer and pulling out a black velvet box. It's not a ring, that much I can tell, but I have a feeling I know exactly what it is.

He snaps the lid open and there, sitting on a soft cushion is a slim silver collar. A small pendant of a rose sits dead center with a ruby shimmering in the light as he moves toward me.

"Will you be mine, Roisin?" he asks, lifting that inquisitive gaze to mine.

I try my hardest to find reasons to say no. Not because I don't want this, but because I'm not sure how to be with someone long-term. To fully give myself to him is something I've contemplated, but not thinking it could be a possibility.

Silence hangs between us. A balance of tension and hope is heavy in the air and with each second that passes, it feels as if we're about to explode.

"I need time to think." I finally offer him the answer that makes him nod. There's a certain sadness that dances in his eyes. "It's not a no. I just need to say goodbye to my demons that keep pulling me backward," I tell him. My voice is scratchy, rough with emotion.

"I know, sweetheart." He finally pulls me into his arms. I so wanted to say yes, but there's something I must do before I can even fathom being with someone like this.

I need to go back to my past and release it. I need to get back the girl I lost and hopefully then, I can finally move on.

"I do want this, and I do want you," I mumble into his shirt. "Before I can commit, I need to do something." I pull away, looking into his eyes. I tell him something I've never said to anyone in my whole life. "I love you, Kian."

"I love you, sweetheart." His response makes me smile. It makes everything I've been through worth the journey. The pain and agony, they're gone.

The only thing that matters is that I'm here with him.

"You're not angry?"

"How could I be? You've made me happy, Rosie," he tells me earnestly. "I am a patient man. When I want something, I can wait, but don't take too long."

"Why? Are you going to kidnap me and lock me up against my will?" I question playfully and his gaze darkens with need.

"Don't tempt me, little one, I'd happily have you bound to my bed forever."

"Mmm, perhaps we should have breakfast before you do that? I'm guessing I'll need my energy for whatever is running through your mind."

This time he laughs, a sound that fills my heart with emotion. Happiness that I've finally found someone who loves me for who I am. He lifts me bridal style in his strong arms and saunters into the kitchen, setting me on the stool at the breakfast bar.

"Eat." It's a one-word order I don't argue with. There's a mound of pancakes, scrambled eggs, and bacon just waiting for us to devour. I can't believe he made them, but then again, I've learned that Kian is a man of many talents, and surprising me is one of them.

KIAN

As soon as I walk into the office, I can't help notice Mikael in a meeting as I pass by our boardroom. I don't recognize the man he's meeting with, but I'm sure it's the client he was telling me about a few days ago. After the night I had, all I wanted to do was crawl back into bed with Rosie, but we both had work to do.

Settling into my office chair, I turn on the computer and open my email. The subject line of one sits in my inbox, above all the others, catching my attention immediately.

ROISIN NOLAN CASE FILE

I ASKED ONE OF MY CONTACTS TO DO A BIT OF DIGGING INTO THIS asshole she grew up with. I'm not sure what I will do with the information yet, but there's one thing I know for certain. I'll be paying the monster a visit.

Opening the message, I tap the attachment. Once it's downloaded, I take a long deep breath before opening the PDF. I scan the briefing, the information, and with every paragraph, my blood turns from simmering to full-on boiling point.

When she was shunned from the asshole's house, she was shoved back into the system, but it's where she ended up that makes my blood run cold. A small town which is five hours north of L.A. where she was schooled, living with two people known for drug and alcohol abuse.

It seems I'm going to have to make two trips out of the city. Just then, my office door flies open and my partner saunters in. "Kian, you look like the cat that's got the cream," he says, settling in the chair opposite my desk.

"She said she needed time," I tell him, noting how he watches me with curiosity.

"And you're okay with that?" he questions incredulously.

I've asked myself this same question over the past few hours, wondering just how fucking whipped I am for this woman.

I'm about to respond when my phone rings. Ignoring Mikael, I pick it up, pressing it to my ear.

"Hey, sweetheart," I answer with a smile.

"Kian, I wanted to ask you—" Her words are cut off when my office door flies open and an old client, a well-known politician, rushes inside, his face contorted in panic.

"Listen, baby, I have to go. You do whatever you want, it's okay. I'll see you tonight, okay?" I don't wait for her to finish, instead hanging up as Mr. Tremil starts speaking.

"I need your help, Ryland," he says, using my last name. "It's a fucking shit show. The woman I asked you to get a background check on?"

"Yeah, Kimberly, or something," I respond, rising to shake his hand, finding it clammy, and I realize he's really fucking panicked.

"She's suing me. I need you to dig up everything you can on her. And I mean everything."

Nodding, I settle behind my computer, tapping at the keys to pull up the file I recall I'd found on the woman who had claimed her daughter was the child of Tremil. We did request blood work, but she refused.

"Did you not get a paternity test like I told you?"

When I glance at the man, I have my answer. Why is it men like this enjoy fucking around? I guess it means more money for me. But this is ridiculous.

"Why is she suing you?"

And that's when my day doesn't go as planned.

It's just hit six in the evening. The sun is just about gone from the sky when I finally rise from my desk. Paperwork is the bane of my existence, it's the one thing I hate to do, but it comes with the job. I realize I haven't heard from Roisin since the earlier call I had to cut short. I'm about to pick up my phone to call her when my office door opens with a whoosh.

"Dude," Mikael says as he strolls into my office. The dark suit and crisp light blue shirt he's wearing along with the silver tie make him look way more distinguished than he normally dresses. "I think there's something you need to see." He sets his laptop on my desk, turning the screen to face me.

A website with images flashing around catches my attention. But it's the heading of the article that causes me to slam my fists against the desktop. "What the fuck is she thinking?" My voice is heavy with frustration when I read the rest of the article. My eyes scan the information she shared, giving away most of my secrets about the photos I've taken, how I meet my submissives, but she thankfully hasn't mentioned Runway or Black Light.

Scrolling down the webpage, I note a few comments and questions about me and who I really am. Her name has popped up a few times in response, but she's not revealed my identity, but she does speak about a few intimate details about us and our relationship.

Two long fucking weeks of happiness she's just decided to plant all over her company's website. There are no photos of me, but it's clear she's kept some things to herself. My blood is running hot through my veins. Anger and confusion at the forefront of my mind.

How she could've done this is beyond me. I've started feeling things for her that I haven't felt in a long time, and now, looking at what she's done angers me more than I thought it could. I knew where she worked. I knew everything about her before she ever confessed to me. But this... This is a situation I need to handle.

"I'll sort it out." I push the computer away from me, not wanting to see more of the damage she's done. Pulling out my phone, I tap out a message for her to be home in ten minutes. "I'm heading out. I'll see you tomorrow," I tell Mikael. Grabbing my keys, I head to the door, leaving my best friend staring at me.

"Are you sure you want to do this? Maybe relax, talk to her tonight?" he offers, causing me to halt in my steps. "You're angry, rightfully so, but maybe there's an explanation. If you go there now, you'll fight, get angry, well... angrier, and perhaps say something you'll regret."

I stare at the door, long and hard, my back to Mikael. He's right, but I can't wait. This is something I need her to retract immediately. Even though there's nothing in her article that outs my name, there are many links to who I really am and if one of the assholes I've fucked over finds it, they'll find me. And that's something I can never let happen.

"Get that article pulled, now," I order my partner before leaving him in my office. He knows what I'm like and I know he'll do a good job of scaring that shit show of a publisher to pull the story immediately.

Anger surges through me as I slip into the driver's seat and start the engine. It's been a long time since I thought about loving someone and I love her. I know I fucking do. And just as soon as I take that step with Roisin, she pulls this shit on me. I should've known this was all a game to her. I wonder how long she's been wanting to experience this whole BDSM scene, and now that she has, she can write about it all she wants.

All those scenes we've played. All the moments I thought were real, were merely a smoke screen. Something she hid behind to get her story. My mind flits to the moment I realized I feel something more for her.

Bound and helpless.

Beautiful and fiery.

"You're so beautiful, your pale, porcelain skin," I coo in her ear. "Your hair that reminds me of a warm sunrise on a summer's day," I whisper over her cheek. My lips, close, but not touching, and I know she can feel the heat of my breath. A small shiver travels over her, making me smile at her reaction to me.

"Master, please," she whimpers when I trail my fingertips over her bare legs. Goose bumps rise on her flesh, making her tremble again as I reach the curve of her breasts. Ignoring her nipples, I circle the curve until my fingers meet the space between both beautiful tits. I move higher, finding her throat, trailing lightly to her lips.

"Suck," I order, pressing my thumb on her plump lower lip. She pulls the digit into her hot wet mouth, suckling on it as if she's working my cock. It throbs in response, wanting to sink into her, but not yet. Once she's wet it to my liking, I pull it from her and press it against her clit that's probably aching for attention. As soon as I make contact she whimpers, her hips rising to meet my touch, but I pull away, causing her to mewl like a hungry kitten. "If you move again I'll spank you," I tell her earnestly, but I know she loves that, so it's not much of a punishment.

I press against her once more, circling the bud until she's begging for release. Her mouth parts on soft shallow breaths as I make her even wetter than she was before. The scent of her arousal is intoxicating as I lean in to swipe my tongue along her slit, tasting the juices that I can't help savoring each time I devour her.

"Would you like to play?"

"Yes, Master," she responds breathily.

I lift the rose-scented candle and tip it until the hot wax trickles over her sensitive nipples, causing her to cry out, tugging on the leather cuffs. I continue a pretty red pattern over her stomach, down toward the beautiful cunt between her thighs. I miss it by an inch and pour wax over her thighs, down to her feet.

The room is warm, but the wax has already hardened when I get back to her pussy, the red drips over her mound, making my woman scream with pained pleasure. I set the candle down and pick up the flogger, allowing the leather strips to tickle her legs, stomach, and tits before I lift it, bringing it down on her with a whooshing swat.

Again and again.

My cock is solid steel behind my zipper when the wax flies off her body and the pink welts appear on the porcelain skin I've come to love seeing marked with my whip, flogger, or anything else I give her. I drop the implement on the floor, shoving my slacks along with my boxer briefs down. Once I'm naked, I don't bother with any more foreplay because I'm about to shoot my load.

I crawl between her spread thighs. Fisting my cock, I position myself at her entrance before slamming in balls deep. The scream I'm gifted with only makes me throb even more.

"Oh God, Master, please," she cries, her moans loud as I pull out and drive back in, harder and faster. There's nothing about love in this moment. I'm fucking her and it's good, so fucking exquisite, her cunt clamps down on my shaft as she squeals her release, drenching me in her juices.

"Such a pretty girl," I tell her, ripping the blindfold from her. She blinks, once, twice, and a third time before she finds me staring at her. I've stopped moving because I want her to see my face when I fill her with my seed. Deep down, I wish I were claiming her, knocking her up

and keeping her as mine. But for now, all I can do is fuck her into submission.

"Please, fuck me," she asks, a smile on her pretty face, and I obey.

"Don't top me from the bottom, sweetheart. I'll fuck you when I'm good and ready," I tell her, swiveling my hips, which makes her head drop back and her eyes roll back. "Look at me, Rosie," I command her attention on me because I don't want her to ever look away from me.

She meets my gaze, then I move. Her body is tight, pulsing around me as I fuck her gently, slow and steady, taunting her. When I reach between us, I press against her nub once more and feel the flurry of pulses from her slick walls. My mouth latches onto her nipple, but I never break eye contact.

"Oh God," she whispers when I bite down on her nipple, tugging it harshly as I fuck her into the mattress. My hips move faster, slamming her into the bed. She's so slim and light, I could fuck her like a little rag doll.

I feel my release skittering down my spine as pleasure zips over me. Her body arches against me as I hit a spot inside her that has her crying out, but my good girl never breaks our eye contact and that's when my balls draw up and I empty myself inside her, marking her from the inside out, and I know this woman is mine. There's no doubt in my mind that I will lay claim, I will collar her, and nothing will stop me.

I'M PULLING UP TO HER BUILDING WHEN I SNAP OUT OF THE HAZE OF that memory. Shoving my car door open, I'm out and making my way to her door before I have time to think. She's going to get punished for giving away secrets that were for her only. This is unacceptable and I do not condone my life being splattered across her company's website.

When I reach the door, I knock twice, harsh and loud. As soon as she appears before me, I'm gripping her throat, shoving her inside and pressing her against the wall with my body.

"You're going to tell me what gave you the right to plant my life, our life, all over the fucking website without talking to me first. And when you're done explaining yourself, you're going to bend over the sofa and I'm going punish you, I'm going to spank you until you're pleading and begging for mercy. I'll revel in watching your big blue eyes shimmer with pretty tears. Then and only then, will I think about fucking you and making you suck your sweet cunt juices from my wet cock. Do we have an understanding?"

Her body shivers at my rage-fueled words as I meet her worried gaze with my angry one.

"I-I it was just..."

"That's not the answer I wanted, Rosie," I bite out, my teeth clenched because I can't deal with having anything about myself being revealed. My life is secret for a reason. What I do, what I enjoy, it's mine to tell, not hers.

"Yes, I understand, Master," she spits out the word and I see red.

Pulling her away from the wall, I walk us to the sofa, bending her over the arm, then ripping the small skirt she's wearing up and over her hips. My hand slaps her ass ten times on each cheek before I let up. Her porcelain skin bright, angry red when I finally step back and breathe.

"Stand."

She moves, watching me like a wounded puppy. I was harsh, but I'm angry.

"Go into the room and wait for me in there. I need to go home and grab a few things. I'll be back in an hour. I need to calm the fuck down before we do this."

ROISIN

"I—"

"I said I'll be back in an hour. And you better be here." He spins on his heel, leaving me alone in my living room wondering what the fuck just happened. I knew I should've told him. Asked him permission. I had a choice, to either accept the demotion she threatened me with or submit the article. I've only had me to think about for so long, when the choice was set before me, I didn't think. Kian was understanding about many things, but this… this was me fucking everything up.

My room is cold, silent, and empty. Even the fact I've turned the heating on doesn't offer me solace. It's not the cold in my home that's causing me to shiver, it's the iciness of not having Kian here to just talk to. Now I know why they say that submissives love differently. Offering yourself to someone so intimately, so wholly, it opens you up to someone in a way that a normal relationship doesn't.

As if he's taken a knife and cut me open, rummaged inside me, and left me to bleed out. Physically, I feel as if I'm dead. I've lost the only person I loved. The one man who not only made me feel beautiful, but made me believe I'm worthy of love.

My past has been dotted with pain, heartache, but I've always been closed off. Not giving myself to anyone in that way for fear of heartbreak, and here I am, broken over a man I'd lied to, then plastered his life for all to see.

I'm not angry at him. I'm angry at myself. Deep down, I know I was wrong. And I can't blame him for leaving. I glance at the time. It's been more than an hour. I don't know if he is actually coming back. I wanted to tell him about my plan, but since he's not here to talk to, I shrug off the fear that I've lost him and decide to pack.

Shoving the clothes into a bag, I take in my bedroom one more time, making sure I have everything. This afternoon I received an email from a lawyer to tell me I've been named as sole heir of a large sum of money, along with the house I grew up in. I wanted to tell Kian, but he didn't give me a chance to explain I've decided to take a short trip, back to the place where life had been stolen from me. I'm about to walk back into a town that condemned me for being a harlot.

I'm not going there for an apology, I'm going there to close off my past.

I'm about to pick up my purse when my phone vibrates. My heart kicks in my chest, attacking me with vengeance. When I unlock the screen, I note it's not a message, merely a notification. There's a photo that's been posted, a new one, on his profile.

As soon as it loads, my breath is caught in my throat. It's me. In black and white, I'm kneeling on the smooth shiny floor. My body is naked, but you can't see anything. As he promised, I'm hidden from sight. No other man can see what he saw.

I look beautiful. I finally see what Kian saw. A girl, shattered, but whole. Learning, journeying on a path that will lead to enlightenment. It will unlock the door I'd kept shut. A submissive, kneeling for her Master. Willing, open, and wanting.

My eyes scan the caption, and tears prick my eyes.

When you open yourself to pain
When you allow yourself to feel
There's nothing that can save you from yourself
But you saved me. And I walked out.

I SHAKE MY HEAD, BLINKING BACK THE TEARS AS THEY BURN MY eyelids. I swallow the emotion down. I should respond. Perhaps I should go to him and ask him what this means. But I don't. I can't do it, not right now. I need to find my closure before I can open the door to him.

Is this an apology?

If it is, he'll have to give me time, just one day before I can even respond. My fingers tingle. They itch to tap out a reply. I shoulder the bag and grab my purse. And as I exit my condo, I know I'll be back soon, because this is my new life. All I need to do is say goodbye to my old one.

On the street, I find people milling about, and for some reason, I feel eyes on me. It's almost as if he's watching me. I shake my head and turn toward the parking lot. I think the drive will give me time to work through my options, and what I want to do. I'll be able to leave the old home that stole my childhood as soon as I've figured out what the lawyer would want from me.

AS I MAKE MY WAY DOWN THE ROAD, MY MIND IS STILL ON KIAN. HE hasn't called yet. There have been no messages as I inch my way out of the city. My small Mini Cooper isn't going anywhere in the late evening traffic. My heart aches, thinking about him. What I did and watching him walk out my door. Even with a promise that he'll return, I didn't believe it.

I'd messed up.

I accept my mistakes.

My phone dings, but I ignore it. I turn up the radio to drown out the incessant ringing and sit back as the traffic starts moving a little faster than before. As the night swallows the day, the cars seem to diminish and I'm able to put my foot down on the accelerator. The faster I go, the more my mind clears.

My favorite band, One Less Reason, screams at me through the speakers, reminding me I should've waited. I should've called him. But I shake my head of those errant thoughts and rather focus on the road before me. I need to do this.

The song changes as Amy Lee and Seether sing *Broken* and I have to blink back the tears that threaten me. Instead, I steer my thoughts to the night I knew I was falling in love with Kian Ryland.

THERE ARE SMALL TEA LIGHT CANDLES AROUND THE ROOM AS WE STEP inside. It's the second time he'll be photographing me and I'm no longer nervous. No. I'm more excited than I've ever been before. He's dressed in a dark shirt that only brightens his brown eyes against the softly tanned skin.

His slacks are black, hugging his thighs as if they've been molded to his body. The man is exquisite. Sexy, alluring, and downright filthy when he wants to be. He doesn't have to lead me to the spot where I drop the robe I'm wearing. The cool hardwood beneath my feet no longer makes me shiver.

I turn to him, facing the camera that sits in the corner. There are times he'll just stand and watch me, but there are other times he gives me instruction as to where he would like me. How I need to pose, bend and twist. Just for him.

The room is warm, and I'm sure he's turned the heating up as we near autumn. I drop to my knees. My long red hair hangs over my shoulders, covering my small breasts from his gaze.

"Tell me, Rosie," he says then. "Give me a poem."

I snap my gaze to his, meeting those impossibly hungry eyes. "I can't just—"

"Yes, you can," he tells me. Lifting the cuffs, he strolls my way. Taking my wrists, he binds them behind my back. My thighs are spread, my body open, presenting him with what he needs. My pussy and my breasts. Even though I'm wearing panties, I feel exposed, and normally that would've scared me, or had me tense, but with Kian, I'm no longer those things.

"Okay," I respond, smiling when he walks back to the camera, taking two snaps before coming toward me, turning me at an angle to get another few shots. I close my eyes, taking a deep breath as I think about my situation, where I am and what I'm doing. "The moon a sliver in the sky, the stars pricking the darkness, but where I am is safe and cared for. You light the fire I've long since forgotten, but you also stoke the kindling until I'm burning from deep within."

It's nothing like my other work. Nothing like the words I've typed out so many times and posted on my social media, but it keeps Kian silent for so long, I turn to face him. He's staring at me as if I'm a stranger, but when he finally stalks forward, I know that's not what he feels.

In his chocolate eyes, there's an emotion dancing wildly, which scares me as much as it gives me strength. He cares for me. And I'm afraid to say there may even be love in his stare. I don't want love, I crave it. I'm hungry for it. But what scares me most is that I'm imagining it.

When the soul is deprived, it creates fairy tales to make-believe that what you see and feel is real. I've never felt any form of affection, but Kian has shown me that in spades since we've been together.

"I told you, sweetheart, you are just magnificent." He takes two more photos, then he steps around the camera and closes the distance between us. Lifting me from the floor, he cocoons me in his warm arms, planting a soft kiss on my forehead.

"That was a short photoshoot," I mumble into his shirt, wanting the heat of his body. As if I can get closer, I burrow myself into his hold. Nuzzling my face into his neck, I breathe in his spicy cologne.

"I can't wait to put you in bed, to hold you close to me, to slide into you and fall asleep with my cock inside you." He smirks down at me as he strolls down the hallway into the master bedroom. He plants me on

the bed, tugging the comforter up and over me. My hands are still bound, but Kian makes quick work on the cuffs and soon I'm freed.

He slips into the bed behind me, naked, warm, and bare. His cock hard as it presses between my ass cheeks. His hips move slow and steady as he slips between my thighs.

"You feel so good," he coos in my ear. There's a tenderness in his movements, in his touch, no longer the harsh commanding Master, but instead the man who's showing me affection. I move my hips, swiveling until his cock slips between the lips of my pussy, and he gently fucks into me.

A small whimper falls from my mouth as he drives into me, torturing me. His cock hitting deep inside, finding the spot inside me that curls my toes as pleasure zooms through me. He pulls out, then slips back in, over and over again. His hands grasp my breasts, twisting my nipples until I'm squealing.

"You're mine."

"I'm yours."

It's a promise. A vow.

There's nothing more I want. It's all here, in this bed. He's all I want. His cock thickens, stretching me painfully and that's what burns me in all the right ways. It heats my blood, it tingles through my veins as my orgasm tightens low in my stomach. Kian circles my clit with his thumb, then presses the hardened nub, causing me to cry out as I find release.

His body shudders behind me. His cock hits that spot and I'm seeing stars when Kian empties himself inside me, filling me with him as I drench him with me. The most intimate I've ever been with any man, I'm with Kian and his body cocoons me in warmth and safety. And I know without a doubt, I am in love.

THE STREETLIGHTS SHINE INTO THE CAR AS I PASS BY EACH ONE. With every mile I get farther away from Los Angeles, I feel the heaviness in my heart at leaving Kian behind. It's been two hours since I've left when I finally pull into a gas station and pull out my phone. I know I have another three hours before I reach the town I spent two long years in.

When I unlock the screen, I find three missed calls and five messages. Tapping the app, I open my messages first and scan the almost desperate words of Kian. I hit dial on his number and press my phone to my ear.

"Where the fuck are you?" he hisses over the phone, causing my body to shiver with anxiety.

"I needed to do something, Kian. Please understand," I plead with him, and his heavy breaths calm from the other end of the line.

"Tell me where you are. I'm coming to get you." He sounds adamant this time, but I wish he'd allow me to do this myself. Knowing the Paulsons are bringing me back to a place I'd rather forget is something that will be emotionally taxing. I realize Kian just wants me safe, but I can never be when I'm still carrying around my past as if it were baggage.

"I can't, Kian. Please, just let me do this one thing. Anyway, I thought you were angry with me?"

He falls silent and I know he's still wanting me there to punish me for the article. But then he shocks the shit out of me when he responds. "I want you here because I can't lose you," he utters.

My heart leaps into my throat, thumping wildly, threatening to choke me. Nobody has ever wanted me. Needed me. But here he is, pleading for me to come back to him.

"I should've told you this when I shoved my way into your place. I love you, Roisin Nolan," he says. There's no hint of humor in his voice. He's being dead serious.

"I-I love you too, Kian."

"I was angry because you told the public about us, about our life. My best friend, Mikael, asked me why I was so angry, and I realized I was jealous. I don't care if people know about me. I thought I did, but I don't." He sighs heavily. "I don't want you being shoved into the public eye. It's not something I could live with."

"Why?" I sass, cheekily.

"Because I want no other person to see you how I see you. Exposed. Vulnerable. Innocent."

I smile at that. His words warm me from my toes all the way to the roots of my red hair. "And what if I told you I love you because you want to keep me safe, but you have to realize, you won't always be there?"

"I'll always be there because when you get your ass back here I'm going to tie you to my bed so you can never leave again." He grunts this time. "Where are you?"

"I got an email this afternoon. I've been called in to a reading of the last will and testament of my previous foster family. The pastor and his wife."

Silence greets me and I wonder if he's hung up, but then I hear the jingle of keys and the click of a door in the background. When I hear an engine purring to life from the other end of the phone, I know he's coming after me.

"Stay where you are. I'll be there within the hour since traffic has died down," he tells me before hanging up and leaving me gaping at a black phone screen.

KIAN

When I got home after leaving Roisin, I got a call from my man who did the background check on her past. He found out the asshole who had violated her died from a heart attack, but I have a feeling it was something else that's being covered up. We've learned how much his wife has covered up to keep his name out of the cops' records.

My body is vibrating with anxiety as I speed down the highway toward where I've tracked Rosie's phone. She doesn't know that I turned on the app on her phone so I can find her anywhere she is. Some might call it obsession. I call it love.

Thankfully the roads are quiet as I make my way to the gas station. I'm still wondering why she would've just left without telling me. I know she mentioned wanting to do this on her own, but there's nothing she's going to do on her own ever. Starting today, Roisin Nolan will have me by her side.

My phone rings through my speakers then, loud and shrill, and a bad feeling settles in my gut about the number that flashes on the screen. I shouldn't answer. But I can't bring myself to ignore it. Tapping the answer button, I wait for the person on the other end to speak.

"Kian." Her voice is so familiar, yet a stranger to me. As much as I prayed for her to call me over the years, she never did. And now that she has, I no longer feel the love I thought I would. No, this time all I experience is frustration that she's calling at a time like this. A time when I should be with the woman I love.

"What do you want?" I question, not offering her a hello. She doesn't deserve it. I wanted joint custody of my daughter and she got the court to approve minimum visitation rights, keeping me from my seeing my child every day. It's been two months since I've seen Cassidy, and my heart aches with every passing day. Her mother has made excuses with every weekend I've made plans to see her and I'm done with her fucking me around. Siobhan has no right to be calling me, or even trying to be nice to me.

"I need your help."

I can't help laughing, the chuckle loud and incredulous, bouncing around me. "That's rich, coming from you Siobhan," I tell her. I know I'm nearing the gas station and I need to hang up before reaching it because I know Roisin is in no state to deal with my ex-wife, and neither am I.

"Listen, I know you're angry with me. I know things ended badly between us."

"Ended? You fucking shut me out and walked out, Siobhan," I bite out angrily, pulling off to the shoulder of the road because my focus is not on the road. The last thing I need is getting into an accident on the way to see my girl.

"I know," she responds, sounding small, almost guilty. I say almost, because my wife has no sense of right and wrong. She was convinced I was the bad guy because I had a dominant streak. I'd suppressed it when she told me she no longer wanted to be spanked, to be blindfolded. Her idea of sex is lying on the bed and moaning at the appropriate times. The years we were married, I gave in and allowed her to make demands.

It only took so long until one night we were intimate when I'd instinctively spanked her. That was it. She raged at me, told me I was sick. She wanted to fight me for full custody, but my lawyer made sure I at least had some visitation rights.

I could never live my life without my daughter, and I know if I didn't fight it, Siobhan would've poisoned Cassidy against me, so there's no way I want to talk to her when I need to be with Roisin.

"Listen to me—"

"Cassidy is sick," she interrupts me with a declaration that stills my fucking heart, turning it cold in my chest.

"What?" I grit out the word. My teeth clench so hard my jaw ticks with frustration. "Tell me what the fuck you mean, Siobhan, and tell me now."

"She's going for tests tomorrow. We're not sure what's wrong yet," my ex-wife tells me easily. "Please, come see her," she pleads.

If there's one thing I recall about the woman I was married to for the younger years of my life, is that she never begs. She'll never allow anyone to force her to ask for help, so if she's calling me to go see my daughter, I can't deny her that.

My heart is torn, ripped down the middle. Either I go back to see Cassidy, or I stay with Roisin. I sit in silence for a moment, mulling over what to do.

"Message me the address." I hang up before she can say her thanks, even though I doubt there would be any. I have to get to my girl. She's probably wondering where I am. I promised I'd go to her, so I will. I'll always keep my promises to her, but I also need to go see my daughter. If this is something serious, I don't know how long I'd have. We don't even know what's wrong with her yet.

Starting the engine, I pull out onto the road once more and put my foot on the gas pedal. The car speeds down the road in the darkness, the only illumination coming from my headlights.

I'm coming, sweetheart, I think. To both my girls, I promise that I'm coming.

~

When I reach the gas station I'm calmer than I was moments after talking to Siobhan. As soon as I park, I find Rosie strolling from the store with a bag of chips and a coke. She looks far too innocent to be sitting in a gas station in the middle of nowhere. I hate having to leave her to do this on her own, but I know I need to get back to my daughter.

The two most important women in my life and I am torn between two opposite ends of the country.

"Hey." She smiles up at me when I saunter toward her. Her cheeks darken with a soft pink and I revel in her beauty. Just her. It's been years since I've loved someone, but with Roisin it's been easy. I never had a chance. She wandered into my life and burrowed herself into my darkness, basking in it, but also offering me her fire, her light.

"Why did you leave without telling me?" I question. My frustration at her being on her own simmers through my veins. Big blue eyes meet mine as she shrugs off the question. "I'm not kidding, sweetheart," I grit out through clenched teeth. "This isn't something you can just shrug off. You're mine," I tell her, hoping it will sink in.

"I know I'm yours, but…" Her words trail off and I feel like bending her over the hood of her car and spanking her ass until she can't sit down.

"But?"

She shakes her head and I'm almost certain she's not going to tell me, but then she turns away, her back to me, against my chest. "I needed to find out what I've been given by the family who tarnished my name in a town where everyone believed I was a slut," she murmurs into the darkness. "It's time to put that to bed, to shove it into my past where it can't come between us."

I grip her shoulders, spinning her to face me. "You should come to me, tell me when something is bothering you. This"—I gesture between us—"isn't going to work if you hide shit from me, Roisin."

She nods slowly, not meeting my gaze that I know is penetrating right through her pain. I pull her into my arms, holding her as if she's about to shatter into a million pieces, and perhaps she is. Maybe when I tell her I need to leave, she'll finally tell me she doesn't want this or me.

What woman would want a man with a child from another woman?

I step back, lifting her chin so she can finally look directly at me and not the ground where she's been staring for a while now. Tears glisten in her eyes, and I know if she blinks they'll fall.

"I need to get back," I tell her reluctantly. Shock mars her pretty face and my heart cracks in my chest at the pain I see registering on her expression. "Something's come up, but I need to tell you about it."

"What is it?" she questions, her voice heavy with concern.

"My ex-wife," I start, swallowing past the lump in my throat. "She called while I was on my way here." I wait for her to slap me, to shout or scream, but she doesn't. She's eerily silent. "My daughter is ill."

This makes Roisin step backward, her ass planting itself on the hood of my car. I reach for her, but she shoves my hand away. "Don't."

"Listen to me, Rosie," I implore, needing to touch her, to hold her. I want to hear her tell me it's okay, but she doesn't. I don't expect her to. "I wanted to tell you—"

"Oh, you did? And when did you plan on telling me, Kian? When I was naked on your floor while you bound me in leather cuffs? Or when I was being fucked by you while you spanked me?" Her voice rises. Thankfully there's no one else around.

Scrubbing my hand over my face, I run my fingers through my hair, tugging on the strands, causing my scalp to prickle. "I just needed time."

"Time? To what? Figure out a lie?"

"No!" My voice booms around us like a foghorn in the silence of the dark night. "I love you, Roisin. Nothing can change that."

"So? What are you doing? Going back to her?"

"No, I don't want to ever go back to Siobhan," I tell her adamantly. This time, I grip her arms so I can shake some sense into her. My frustration is now skyrocketing through me, making my blood boil at the woman who's suddenly come back into my life and forced me to remember I have a child after she spent years keeping her from me.

"Then what, Kian? I can't do this back and forth. I can't love you if you're just going to do what everyone else in my life did to me." Her voice is so quiet, so filled with pain that I feel it right down to my gut.

Shaking my head, I respond, "I'm not leaving you. Siobhan walked out. Even though I see Cassidy every few weeks, I no longer love my ex-wife." This time I drop my head, feeling sadness take over the anger and frustration.

"I feel fragile right now," she confesses, lowering her gaze to the gravel beneath our feet. I want her eyes on me. I want her to look at me, how serious I am about us, about the life I want with her.

"And I'm sorry I've just added to it," I tell her, dropping to my knees before her. "I never wanted to hurt you and I was afraid if you knew about my daughter right away, before I even knew when I'd get to see her again, that you'd walk out and..." It's my turn to trail my words into silence. Admitting I want her is one thing, confessing I love her is another, but finally voicing that I would not survive without her? That scares me shitless.

"And?" she prompts, looking right at me, and I wonder if she can see how I feel. *Can she look into my soul and recognize how lost I would be without her?*

"Roisin, I've loved before, that's not something I can deny, but the thing between us"—I sigh—"it's not something I've felt before. You're not just a woman I love. Not just a submissive, you've become an all-consuming obsession."

She sucks in a shocked breath at my words. Her hands fall to my shoulders, holding on to me as if she's about to collapse. "Please stand," she pleads and I obey. She lifts her eyes, meeting mine, then she leans up on her tiptoes, pressing a soft kiss to my mouth. She tastes like sugar and innocence. An intoxicating combination for me.

I graze my teeth over her lower lip, sucking it into my mouth. Biting down on the plump flesh, I elicit a whimper from her, and I delve my tongue into her warmth.

Her arms wrap around my neck as she attempts to climb up my body. It's as if I'm her lifeline and she's holding on with all her strength. When I finally pull away, I'm hard, and Rosie is panting, needy, and I'm certain if I put my hand between her thighs she'll be wet for me.

"I want you to get in the car. Do not stop until you reach town," I tell her. "When you get there you will send me a message to tell me exactly where you are. I'll come to you." It's a promise. As soon as I get back I'll find out what's wrong with Cassidy, and then I'll come for my woman.

Nothing is going to keep me away from Roisin.

"Shouldn't you stay with your daughter?" she rasps, her eyes wide with questions I can't answer right now. I should've told her before this. I should've offered up my secrets I held onto, but I didn't. Thankfully, she isn't running for the hills.

"I should. But I'm not sure what's wrong with her yet. When I get back, I'll hopefully have more answers." Reaching up, I trail my knuckles over her cheek. The tender moment passes when she nods and turns away.

"Okay, well, I better get going," she says, her voice faraway, and I feel her slipping from me, inch by excruciating inch. I never planned on falling in love with her. It was meant to be fun, a few scenes, teaching her how this life works, but in the process, I gave her my heart.

"I love you. Don't you forget that," I tell her, talking to her back.

She glances over her shoulder at me, offering me a small, shy smile. One I recall seeing the first time I met her. "And I love you," she says, slipping into the driver's seat and shutting the door. The engine roars to life, and I watch as she pulls out onto the darkened road, leaving me staring at the red lights as they disappear into tiny pinpricks.

There's a heaviness in my chest that I attempt to squash, but it doesn't relent. Seeing her leave is not something I was prepared for. Even though I know I'll find her again, there's something so final about seeing her car vanish in the distance.

I turn back to my own car and get inside. As soon as I'm on the road again, I allow my focus to stray from Rosie to Cassidy. She needs me, and I can't stop the fear from creeping up in me. I have to offer her strength, no matter what is wrong, but the thought of anything happening to my little girl, it pains me so much I can't breathe.

It's been a few weeks since I've seen her. Siobhan took her on a vacation to Disney World. I saw a few photos she sent, but I never got to experience Cassidy's joy for myself.

I think back to the first time I saw her and my heart aches. A baby that could've fit in a shoe box. She was the tiniest thing. Her big brown eyes, with a small button nose, and the moment her tiny hand wrapped around my finger I was a goner. Nobody, not even Siobhan could've made me feel so proud. Now, she's a little girl. Old enough to walk, talk, and call me daddy.

Her sass is on par with her mother's. And I'm sure she gets the feisty personality from my ex-wife. She's nothing short of amazing. With every mile that takes me closer to her, all I can do is pray there's nothing seriously wrong with her.

ROISIN

As soon as my car entered the small, forgotten town, I felt the agony of what had happened to me. The laughter and sneers. The angry words spewed at me. But nothing compares to the moment I pull up to my childhood home. A place I felt protected in for years, but also the place where that security was stolen in a moment of anger. In a fit of rage and close-minded judgment, I was broken.

There are no cars in the driveway when I stop mine at the sidewalk. I sit staring at the building, each window black in the darkness of the moonless night. A shiver trickles down my spine as if there's someone trailing a finger over my cold skin.

Picking up my phone, I hit dial on his number. Kian asked me to let him know when I arrived. I'm still in two minds about his confession about a daughter. Having an ex-wife isn't something that would bother me, but a child is a connection between two people. Nothing can break that, not even love.

"Sweetheart," he answers. I can hear the smile in his voice and I picture his eyes crinkling in the corners as he says the word. "Are you okay?"

"I am," I respond, my voice croaky from all the emotions

slamming into me at once. This could be the last time I speak to him. Depending on what happens with his daughter, I won't be known again for my so-called *evil* ways. I also don't want to be known for stealing a man from his daughter, or for being in the middle of a relationship, even if it is over.

Not that I was evil. But when I left this shithole, everyone thought it. They were told lies about what I did. The ugliness of people, humans hurting each other with untruths just to ensure their name, who they are, stays sparkly and clean.

Nobody would've believed me anyway. It was my word against his. The beloved pastor of the town. The man who wore his religion like a uniform. Everyone thought he was a saint. But I knew better. Behind closed doors, he was nothing but a wolf in sheep's clothing.

"I meant what I said, Roisin," Kian says, breaking through the agonizing thoughts and memories that take hold of me.

"I know."

"Don't ever doubt my feelings for you, sweetheart," he assures me. There's conviction in his tone, which makes me want to believe him. I want to hold onto his promise, but I've learned throughout my life than men make promises they can't always keep.

"I have to go, need to find a hotel in this shithole," I tell him, not wanting to talk about the impending storm that's about to hit our lives. Dark thoughts grab hold of me, threatening to choke the life out of me.

"Okay, I'll call you in the morning," he tells me. "I love you." Three words I've wanted to hear all my life echo through the speaker of my phone. They sound sincere. I don't doubt he loves me. I doubt I can be enough.

"I know."

I hang up before he can respond.

Sighing, I start the car and drive down toward the main center of town. There's a small motel on the other side of the main street and I pull into the parking lot.

I feel tired. Exhausted from what I'm about to face. Unsure of why they've dragged me back here. After all the evil that took place, I should just leave, but as always curiosity keeps me here.

As soon as I have the keys to my room, I slip inside and flop onto the bed, not bothering to change into more comfortable clothes. Curling up on the soft mattress, I close my eyes and pray for something, anything to save me from tomorrow's meeting with the lawyer.

"MS. NOLAN." THE MAN SMIRKS, AND I WONDER IF HE REMEMBERS me. I know his face. Mr. Mathieson was one of the Paulsons' best friends. He'd visit almost weekly, having dinners, drinking wine, before getting drunk on the porch and needing a cab home.

"It's been a long while, Mr. Mathieson," I tell him, settling on the chair opposite his large dark oak desk. The office itself is brightly lit from the sun streaming through the window behind him, but the furniture in the room reminds me of an old museum. Everything looks to be ancient in the sunny room.

"It has been. I trust you're well?" he says, shuffling papers on his desk, which looks like a bomb slammed into the documents, leaving them strewn haphazardly all over the space.

"I am. I'm unsure as to why I've been called here, though." My response is confident, yet filled with confusion, causing him to glance up.

"Well, the Paulsons both passed on in a tragic accident only four months ago," he says, shaking his head as if I should feel anything. I don't. "They've left final wishes for you, Roisin," he tells me, sifting through the pages. When he finds what he's looking for, he places it closer to where I'm seated.

I lift the documents, scanning my eyes over the wording. Sure enough, they've left me the old dilapidated house as well as some money, which is nothing to get excited about. My chest burns with anger.

"I don't want anything from them," I tell him, dropping the folder back onto his desk. "You can take it and donate it to charity or something."

His shocked expression makes him look like he's about to explode. His face reddens as he sputters his words. "But you can't just deny the inheritance."

"I can. I haven't seen them since I was sixteen when they shoved me back into the system. Why would they leave anything to me after what happened?" I question heatedly.

"Ah, well, this may explain it better." He hands me an envelope, which I'm certain is a letter filled with shit from either of the Paulsons. I don't want it, but I'm intrigued.

I rip the flap open, pulling out a page that has his scrawl all over it.

Little Rosie,

It's been a rather long time since we've seen you. But make no mistake, we miss you in the house. It's so silent. So dreary without your bright red hair. I made a mistake. I realize it now. My anger took hold of me and I should have never done what I did. Punishing you for your teen curiosity was wrong and I hope you'll accept our apologies in the form of the home you once loved.

You may hate us. You may even blame us for everything that happened, and you're right to do so, but you have to understand, my religion was the only thing I knew to be true. I had fulfilled my calling.

If you're reading this, then I'm no longer on this earth.

Please take what we've left you as a token of our love.

Pastor Paulson

Glancing at Mr. Mathieson again, I laugh. I laugh so hard my stomach hurts. He stares at me as if I've lost my mind. Of course, I may have.

"Like I said, I don't want anything. Sell it, burn it to the ground," I tell him once more. Rising from my seat, I rip the letter into tiny pieces, dropping them on his desk. I snatch my purse and turn toward the door. "Oh, and one more thing, I trust that nobody from this shithole of a town will call me again. Nothing will make me want anything from any of you."

Shutting his office door, I stalk out of the building and into the warm sunshine. I haven't looked at my phone since last night. I turned it off, shoving it in my purse, not wanting to hear from Kian, or anyone else for that matter.

I slip into my car and make my way out toward the pier. It's the only place I feel like being right now. When I arrive, I park the car and head toward the water. I breathe deeply, reveling in the fresh air. The waves crash and break angrily against the wooden poles that are sunk deep beneath the surface.

My mind flits back to the night I was *punished* by Paulson while his wife watched on. She did nothing to help. She was the one who spurred him on. *Doing God's work.*

"Is this what you do when we've taught you to be a good girl?" he spits in my face, causing me to wince at the venom of his words. "You're an evil child. The devil is within you," he tells me angrily. His large hand wraps around my throat as he pins me to the bed. The photos are lying on the mattress beside me.

"Martin," she says from behind him. "Maybe she's been doing this with people." Her voice is dripping with concern, which causes her husband to glare at me with enough rage that I'm certain if looks could kill I'd be dead beneath him.

His body is heavy as he leans in, his face inches from mine. "Is this the shit you do with boys at school?"

I attempt to shake my head, choking out a no*, but he just laughs at me. His other hand comes down hard on my cheek, causing it to sting painfully. When I blink, tears trickle from my eyes and pool in my ears. My body is shaking as I try to twist away from him, but I can't move away.*

He shoves me over the edge of my bed. The window is shut, the scent of his cigarettes hangs heavy in the air and I fight the need to retch. A whooshing sound comes from behind me and I know I'm about to get punished. His large hand presses the middle of my back, holding me in place and I can't move.

"I'm sorry, please don't do this," I beg, but I know it's no use because his eyes were black as night and he's not thinking clearly. He tugs at my underwear, ripping them from my slim hips and I'm bared to his evil gaze.

Without further warning, my skin burns from the leather licking at it. Again, and again. I don't know how many times he does it, how many times the belt hits my sensitive flesh because I'm lost in the agony of it. Then I feel it, the gentle trickle of blood as it drips down my thighs.

The loud clank of the belt falling on the floor makes me breathe easier, but as soon as I think the punishment is over, I realize it's far from it.

His hardness against my thigh. He bucks his hips against me again and again. "I'll ensure you are pure again," he promises. I don't know what he means, but he slaps me again and again until I'm sure I'll be bruised tomorrow and won't be able to go to school.

"Please," I croak out again, but he's lost in a fit of rage as he presses his body against mine and I'm certain he's enjoying this far too much. Bile rises in my throat, and I turn my head before it fills my mouth and lands on the comforter I'm being pressed into.

"Stupid little bitch, get the devil out of you," he rages, then suddenly he rocks his hips faster and faster before grunting like an animal. I feel wetness on my bare thigh before he releases me and storms from my

room. His wife, Marlena, shakes her head sadly before closing my bedroom door, leaving me to curl into the fetal position and cry myself to sleep.

Shaking my head of the memory, I blink, allowing the tears to stream down my cheeks. It wasn't the only time he tried to *cure* me. Even though he never violated me psychically, he broke me mentally. There was nothing I could do but endure it. I had no money to run away. I had nothing and they made sure I didn't.

Which makes me wonder how they would think that after their death I'd ever forgive them for what they did to me. For taking a young girl and turning her into an angry, scared woman. It took me years to overcome being fearful of everyone who came into my life and offered me a smile.

I'd believed there were no good people out there. When they said something nice, I'd believe they were out to hurt me later on. My second foster home was just as bad, only they made sure I learned that sex was something I could use to get things I need.

I watched how women were treated as payment. Dana would fuck any man who walked into the house as long as he could provide alcohol or drugs. Her husband would watch, he'd chuckle and call her names. And deep down I knew it was wrong. But I couldn't leave until I had saved up enough money that I stole from them.

As soon as my eighteenth birthday arrived, I walked out of the horrors of that rundown house and made sure nobody ever hurt me again.

Now, I need to decide what to do about Kian. Do I stay with him and be a stepmother to his daughter? Or do I allow him to try to build a life with her and her mom?

He said he wants me. He told me he loves me, and that he wants a forever with me, but there's nothing stopping him from walking out after a few years when he realizes he would rather be with his ex-wife. Shaking the fear from my mind, I turn on my phone and wait for it to boot up.

It dings wildly with calls, messages, and even a few emails from him. I don't know where to start, so I open his messages all asking me where I am, if I'm okay. His voicemails are not any different. Except he's ordered me to call him immediately.

I hit dial, closing my eyes, waiting for the pain.

"Baby girl, you're going to get such a fucking spanking when I get my hands on you," he answers. No *hello,* just a threat that heats my blood with need.

"I'm sorry, I had the meeting this morning and I needed time. This place holds nothing of me, or for me anymore," I tell him earnestly. And I know I mean it right down to my core. Even though I believed it a long time ago, being back here has reminded me why I left in the first place. I was born for more than what I experienced here. I was stronger than any of the people who had treated me like a disease.

"Does that mean you're coming home to me?" he questions.

I ignore his question and respond with one of my own. "How is your daughter?"

He sighs, and my heart stills, waiting for his response. Silence has never been my friend. I hold my breath, willing him to give me good news. Pleading without words for him to tell me it's nothing serious. That she's going to be fine. As much as I want to be with him, I know she is more important than my neediness.

I open my eyes, watching the water as it attacks the pier I'm standing on. It's beautifully violent. Just like my feelings for Kian, they're borderline obsessive.

"She's not doing so well," he tells me sadly, causing my blood to run cold with fear for both me and the little girl I know nothing about. The fear in his voice chokes me. A man so strong and commanding all the time, broken down by heartache.

"What do you mean? What's wrong with her?"

Once more, he doesn't respond immediately. My mind runs

away with everything that could possibly be wrong. Tears sting my eyes, and I blink them away.

"Kian?" I question, his name a whisper and I wonder if he's heard me over the loud crashing of the waves below me. Another long sigh, and then he utters the words that cause me to drop to my knees.

KIAN

The hospital is cold. The smell assaults my nostrils as I enter the main doors. I've always hated places like this. I've avoided them most of my life. Even when my parents died, I didn't see them. I hid away from the agony that seems to hang in the air of a hospital ward.

Now, as I make my way down the hallway, I realize I'm breaking all my rules. I don't feel angry for it, though. I'm here for my little girl. The elevator spits me out on the fourth floor. Turning the corner, I find the woman who left me almost five years ago.

"Kian," she says, her body visibly vibrating with fear and stress. I can feel her anxiety because it seems to emanate from her like a perfume. "I'm sorry to have called you so late."

"Sorry? This is something I should've known about long before the moment you decided to pick up the phone." My voice is cold, icy as I retort my response.

"I know, I was wrong," she admits with a nod, settling in the chair. She doesn't look at me. I want answers, but I don't press it, because I'll lose my shit right here in this hospital if she tells me it was my fault. The night she packed her bags was all her. I never cheated, I gave her everything a woman could want, but she still walked out. I wasn't good enough for her. That was her decision.

"How is Cass?"

"She's having tests done now. They need to find out if it's operable. The tumor is in her stomach. If it hasn't spread, the doctor said she has an eighty percent chance of recovering fully," she tells me.

Cancer.

Fuck that shit.

It's not taking my daughter.

My thoughts are filled with how many experiences I've lost with my baby girl as she was growing up. The moments I am afforded are timed, limited to the park near the house she stays in with her mother, or a small café a couple of blocks away. Siobhan has taken a lot from me, and it's time she gives it back. I feel like a goddamn stranger sitting here in the hospital when it's my child in there. She's a part of me.

"There's nothing I can say that will make what I did okay," she offers me with sadness in her tone, but I don't believe it's an apology. Nothing this woman does is for the good of anyone other than herself.

"You know, Siobhan, for years I waited for you to give me the opportunity to be a proper father. I never hurt you, and I've never hurt Cass, she's my pride and joy. Just because we grew into different people doesn't mean I'm the bad guy here. There were so many nights I prayed you'd call, that you'd tell me you just lost your mind," I tell her, not looking at her. Instead, my focus is on the wall before us, on the cream paint shining in the bright fluorescent lights overhead. "But I've realized you never will. I moved on. I finally let you go."

"You can't be serious." She gasps, turning her head my way. I still don't look at her. I know if I do, I might do something I'll regret, like tell her where to shove her apologies.

"I'm very fucking serious." There's no debating that I'm no

longer the young man in love with a woman who fucked me over. Siobhan was the one who stole my heart, the older woman. She's three years my senior, and sometimes I wonder how that's possible because I feel so much older than her.

"Kian—"

"I met someone," I tell her, knowing there is never going to be a good time to tell her this. "I'm in love with her. I plan to marry her. However, if you try to take my daughter away from me after this because I've moved on, then I suggest you ensure you're ready for a fight." I finally turn my gaze her way. My eyes land on her hand, finding a large sparkling diamond sitting on her ring finger.

Chuckling, I shake my head.

"I should've known."

"It's not what you think," she tells me. "This wasn't a call for John and I to take Cassie from you, and it wasn't to hurt you. I spoke with Jonathan and he's made me see how I wronged you."

"So it took another man who's playing daddy with my daughter to convince you to call me?"

She looks away, and I'm certain I see pained guilt on her expression. We sit in silence for a long while before Siobhan speaks again. "I hated you because I was scared of your lifestyle," she admits after so long.

"I didn't ever hurt you."

"I know, I know." She sighs. "I've just always been wary of anything that wasn't what you would call *vanilla* and when you got more into wanting to blindfold and whip me, I just freaked out. I didn't understand the fascination. I still don't. I judged you as a man, as a partner."

I nod, knowing it's something not everyone would understand. But I was married to her for years before I finally found my Dominant side. And yes, once I unlocked that part of me, I couldn't put him back into the closet he'd been hiding in.

"It didn't matter what I wanted sexually, Siobhan, you took my daughter and held her hostage from me. I've missed out on most of her life because of your fears."

"I was worried she'd see things that—"

"Fuck you," I bite out, rising from the seat. I want to punch the wall. I want to hit something, my blood slowly boiling beneath the surface at her words. It didn't matter who I was, what I wanted. My daughter would never suffer from my needs.

"I'm sorry, Kian. I really am."

I'm about to respond when the doors whoosh open and an older man in a white coat stalks toward us. He offers me a nod, then glances at Siobhan.

"Ms. O'Connell," he says, "we've done the preliminary tests and we're certain that your daughter can be operated on. She's strong, and the cancer hasn't spread. We've caught it early," he tells us both, then glances at me. "We are ninety percent sure we've caught this before it does any damage."

"That's good, right?" Siobhan looks at him, then drags her gaze my way as if asking for my opinion. I want my daughter to live, to be healthy and happy.

"Yes, what do you need from us?"

"You're the father?" he questions me, shoving his glasses up his nose.

"I am." My affirmation makes him smile.

He stalks by us, crooking his finger, telling us to follow him. "Good, we've confirmed her blood type is A-positive, so we'll need to ensure we get a donation from whomever is a match," the doctor informs her.

"I'm a match for Cassidy," I tell him, knowing that I'm A-positive.

He nods, making a note on the clipboard. We trail behind him as we're led into a room where a nurse waits for us. I settle on the bed and wait.

It's been the longest few weeks and knowing I can't go to

Roisin to talk to her makes me even more antsy. I understand her trepidation, and all I can hope is that she accepts my invite.

"I hope you'll find happiness," Siobhan says while the nurse is hooking me up to the blood bag. "Is she a good person? The girl who's caught your attention?"

"She is." My response is short. I meet her inquisitive gaze but don't offer more about the woman I'll soon be marrying. Rosie thinks she can run and hide, but she doesn't know that it doesn't matter where she is in this world, I'll find her. I'll claim her.

"I'm sure Cassidy would like to meet her." Siobhan's words cause me to snap my gaze up to hers. "She wants to spend more time with you."

"She asked for me?" I question.

"She does, Kian. I don't lie to her about you. Every time you bring her home to me she asks me when you'll stay. I haven't explained our situation, but she has a photo of you on her bedside table."

"So, what does this mean? I finally get joint custody of my daughter? Or is this some game you're playing?" My questions make her silent and I wait with bated breath. There's nothing between us but the need for truth. For something more than she's ever offered me. I want to be a father more than I ever wanted to be a CIA agent. I want Rosie and me to have a family, but I'll never be able to replace my daughter with anyone else.

She shakes her head, her face lit up in a way I've never seen before. At least, not since our wedding when we'd promised each other lies. "I'm not leaving again. Jonathan and I will be living in California," she tells me and my chest fills with happiness I can't fathom. Yes, Roisin makes me happy, but this is something else. I recall the moment I held Cassidy as a baby again, her small body, her tiny hands and feet. That scrunched up face made me feel a love that is indescribable.

"And I'm allowed to spend time with my daughter as a parent? Not some fucking once a month visitor?" My voice sounds cautious when I ask her the question I've been wondering since the moment I heard her voice on the phone.

"You are," the woman I used to love smiles and nods.

It's a promise.

One I'm holding her to.

ROISIN

"She's your wife, Kian," I tell him in frustration. "And your daughter? You can't walk away from that. They need you right now." My voice cracks immediately when I realize I'm pushing him into the arms of another woman. Not just any woman, but one who has his child. There's no competing with that.

"I don't love her, Roisin," he confirms once more, but this isn't about loving her or not. This is about him needing to give his support to the two women who need him right now, and that's not me.

Once again, my past rears its ugly head and I know I'm fucked. I can never get over this. It's been weeks, almost two months that we've been together, and in that time, Kian has shown me that love exists. He's broken down the walls I had built up around myself and offered me something I never thought I'd have. And if this is the end, then I am thankful for that. However, if it's not the end, then I know he'll come back to me. How does that old saying go? If you love something let it go, if it comes back, then you'll know it was meant for you.

"I know what it's like coming from a broken home," I tell him, meeting his gaze once more. I can't do this, and he can't convince me to let him stay. Rising from my sofa, I pull my front door open to be met with the woman who's back in Kian's life along with a pretty little girl who's the spitting image of her father.

My heart aches. It cracks in my chest just a little more at the sight of her big brown eyes that match her father's.

"I-I, uhm," the woman mumbles.

"We have to go?" Kian questions her from behind me.

She nods, glancing at the little girl, and my heart aches. It cracks open wide and I have no response to offer. I can't even greet them. His ex-wife smiles then turns to leave and I know she'll be waiting for him downstairs.

Kian steps around me. Gripping my shoulders, he leans down so we're eye to eye. "This isn't over, not by a long fucking shot, Roisin," he vows, but all I can do is nod. And then he's gone.

THE DOORBELL DINGING DRAGS ME FROM THOUGHTS OF LOSS. As much as I want to believe it's him, I know it can't be. When I pull the door open, I find my best friend who I haven't spoken to in weeks on the threshold.

"Greer," I mumble her name.

"I've been thinking," she says in response, squeezing her way into my home. There's one thing about Greer. She doesn't apologize, but she doesn't take no for an answer. If I'd told her I'm not interested in company tonight, she would've barged into my home anyway.

"What are you doing here?"

"Since you and Mr. Hot and Kinky are doing naughty things, I want to know more." She flops on the sofa, her gaze finally meeting mine. "Oh God, what's wrong?" She's on her feet in seconds and I flinch, wondering how awful I must look. I've been crying all day, all night, and I am sure my face is swollen and red.

"Nothing," I tell her, knowing she'll keep pressing until I've confided in her. "I wasn't sure you were still talking to me after your—"

"Misunderstanding," she interrupts me. "I judged you. Unfairly, I might add. Now tell me, what's going on?" She grabs my hands, pulling me onto the sofa beside her. Her expression is filled with worry at the state I'm in.

"Kian's ex-wife is back," I tell her. The shocked gasp of my best friend reminds me there's so much she doesn't know. So much that happened over the past few weeks that she wasn't here for. With nobody else to talk to, all I had was Kian.

"Is he leaving you for his ex?" she asks, lifting one golden eyebrow in question.

"No, nothing like that, it's just…" I allow my explanation to filter into nothing because I can't bring myself to tell her. To even talk about her hurts my heart.

"Rosie, tell me what's going on."

"He has a daughter." The words spill out, frustration evident in my voice. I meet my best friend's gaze again and see all the questions I have for Kian swimming in her eyes. "She's sick, and his ex called him to be there. I don't know the whole story."

"Fuck," she mumbles, sitting back, her face frozen in shock. "And he broke up with you?"

"No, that's just the thing," I respond. "He wants me, he told me he loves me, wants a life with me." This confession causes her to snap her gaze to mine. Her brows pinch together in confusion. "I just didn't want to be the reason his daughter comes from a broken home."

"It was broken long before you came along, Rosie," she tells me something I thought of last night. When I got home, Kian and I spoke, he fell asleep on the sofa, and I sat up watching him. Not creepy at all, but I couldn't bring myself to leave him and go into the bedroom alone.

"I know. You're right."

"I'm always right, girlfriend." She giggles. "Look, if he confessed his feelings even after he learned his daughter is ill, and his ex-wife came back into this life. Then surely that means something? And I mean, the bitch is getting married to some other douchebag. It's not like she's going to try get Kian back."

I nod slowly.

My mind has been filled with so many excuses, which now make no sense, I didn't think about her engagement announcement to Kian.

"And his best friend is so adamant of his feelings for you, and he would know—"

"Woah, wait, hold on," I interrupt her, looking at the guilty, yet satisfied smile on her face. "His best friend?"

"Yeah," she responds, not meeting my penetrating stare. "Mikael came to the office looking for you last week. I told him you were away for a little while and we got to talking," Greer gushes. "He's so handsome, and he's also a Dominant. He likes all that…" She waves her hands in the air, but I really don't want to think about what my best friend and Mikael were getting up to.

"Okay, wow," I finally respond, unsure of what else to say about her confession. "And you're okay with all this?" I ask, curious to hear why she had changed her mind. I know that as much as she enjoys flirting and playing the field, she's also strong-minded and no man would've convinced her otherwise.

"Well, after I left here, I was curious. I went online, and I managed to talk to other women, who are in this… life," she tells me. "It wasn't something I wanted for myself, at least not until I realized how much strength it takes to give yourself to someone so wholly."

"So you're not disgusted with me anymore?" I chance the question at her, hoping that our fight is in the past.

"I was never disgusted with you, more like overly concerned. Seeing you so willing to give yourself to a stranger worried me. At the time, he was nothing more than a name on a website. And, I guess I freaked out because I didn't understand it. I feel terrible, and I didn't know how to come to you and apologize."

"It's okay."

"No, it's not, you were just trying to look out for me." I pull her into a hug, the comfort calming me, and I wish Kian were here because I want him here, I need him here.

"Now," Greer says, her voice stern and serious. "You're going to go to this party with me next Friday," she informs me, pulling up the email, and I note that she's been invited by Mikael. A party at Black Light. "And you should have an invite as well."

"I don't—"

"Have you checked your mails?" she questions me incredulously as if I'm an errant child.

Sighing, I pick up my phone, unlocking the screen and opening my app. There, right at the top, is the reminder about the dinner. The invite I ignored, which only seems to be haunting me now. It's a formal event, and I have nothing to wear.

"Don't you even attempt to find an excuse. You have two weeks to plan. We'll go shopping, find you something sexy to wear."

"Why would he invite me?"

"Because he loves you." She tells me this as if I should just suck it up and go with it. "Now what are we drinking this evening?" She giggles excitedly, rising from the sofa. Greer heads into my kitchen. I hear the clinking of glasses as she rummages around the room. The hiss of the fridge alerts me she's found the bottle of white wine I had chilling.

When she returns to the living room with two glasses, I know we're in for a girls' night.

"Pizza?" I question, scrolling through my phone to find the number for the local delivery place.

She settles on the sofa, crossing her legs on the cushions, and opens the wine before filling both our glasses. "You know it."

Once I've ordered, we sit back and talk, and it feels good to have someone to share the past few months with.

My mind flits to Kian every so often during the evening. I can't stop it. There's nothing I can do to hide my feelings for him. But I told him two weeks, to give me time, and to also allow him time with his daughter. After four years of not seeing her, I'm sure they need to grow as father and daughter.

The relationship is volatile at best when it comes to parents and their children, but when your child is ill, I can't imagine the strain it puts on parents. Deep down, I wish that one day I will be able to give him that. To give him a family. Shaking my head, I remind myself I'm getting ahead of where we are right now.

"Are you listening to me?" Greer questions, causing me to snap out of the worried haze of thoughts that seem to take over me.

"Yeah, sorry, I'm just—"

"Worried about him?"

I nod at her question.

"I get that."

"Tell me about Mikael," I offer, hoping to change the subject.

She hops onto her knees excitedly, like a child who's just been told we're going toy shopping. "Well, he asked me to go for dinner one night, and it was the best date I've been on in ages." Her eyes sparkle when she talks about him and I'm certain that's what Kian does to me. "Anyway, we played our first scene two days ago."

"Oh my God, tell me everything. Well, not all the dirty bits, just, you know."

This has her giggling and I finally allow myself to feel happiness that my best friend has found someone who she likes. And I can tell from the smile on her face as she recollects some intimate details that she's falling and she's definitely falling hard.

"Anyway, it's just all so new."

"It is," I agree, remembering the first time Kian and I played. There's nothing like being under someone else's control. Having them gift you pleasure when they feel it's time for you to receive it. But it's not only that, it was letting go of all the inhibitions that would normally hold me back.

That's what he gave me.

Freedom.

"What if we had a double wedding?" she questions excitedly and my head snaps up in shock. "I mean, like clearly you love Kian and I think I may be in love for the first time in my life. Mikael is everything." She grins like a crazy person.

"We weren't talking about weddings," I retort, finishing my wine, setting the glass on the table before picking up our second bottle of the evening.

"Doesn't matter. There will be a wedding when Kian realizes how amazing you are and comes rushing here to steal you away and lock you in his dungeon."

That makes me laugh, a full belly chuckle that has Greer giggling. And for the first time in a week, I feel like she might be right.

KIAN

The silence of the garden is welcome. I didn't think she'd come, but for the most part I thought she'd at least offer me a response. I lift the glass to my lips, sipping the harsh liquid. People all around me chat to friends, partners, and some I know from Black Light, but I'm alone.

I think about her every day. Each hour that's passed is one more I don't have Roisin in my arms. She gave me space, which I'm forever grateful for, but I didn't want it. Cassidy is my life, she always will be, but so is Rosie.

I've called, messaged, emailed. Everything short of stalking her again like an obsessed asshole, but I can't force her to want to be with me.

I'm happy and sad at the same time. Both emotions fight for dominance within me, but neither wins out. My daughter is going to be okay, the cancer was removed in time, but the celebration is short-lived since I have no one to call my own.

Siobhan told me she realizes that Cassidy needs a father, and even though my ex-wife has now moved on and is engaged, I'll still be able to see my daughter every other weekend. Baby steps with her. Thankfully, I can say that as much pain as she put me through, she's given me a gift I could never refuse. More time with my child.

I make my way back inside. Mikael finds me as soon as I reach the bar. He's dressed in a navy blue pinstripe suit that is tailored for his body shape. The silver dress shirt he's wearing makes his eyes seem more blue than green. Even though he doesn't have a tie on, he still looks like he's heading to a business meeting.

"Kian," he says, slapping me on the shoulder.

"What's up?" I question as he settles beside me on the high stool. "I didn't think you'd be here tonight, since you don't like coming here for events either," I tell him, knowing he hates these fancy dress parties as much as I do.

My best friend without a woman on his arm is a strange thing to see. Since I've known him, there's never been a time when I haven't seen him with some beautiful woman draped over him.

"Taking it easy tonight," he tells me. "I met someone," he offers. Those eyes that regard me with amusement shine with something else.

"Oh?" This piques my interest as I meet his gaze.

"Yeah, she's beautiful, man," he informs with a rumbling chuckle. Then lifts his glass to someone behind me. It's when I turn around that my heart beats wildly in my chest, like a drum sounding loud in my ears.

There, standing beside a beautiful blonde who's looking right past me, is Roisin.

"This is Greer."

The woman who owns my heart smiles sweetly at me.

I cast a glance at the girl beside her, nod, then offer my hand.

"I've heard so much about you, Kian," Greer says in her soft voice. "Look after her," she tells me, her tone no longer friendly. "And if you hurt her, I'll ensure you feel pain every time you try to take a piss."

I can't help chuckling at her little threat, but something tells me not to fuck with this chick because there's no amusement in her tone.

"Okay," Roisin says, nudging her head toward the patio doors that lead outside.

Like a puppet on a string, I follow without complaint. I can't believe she's here. She's dressed like a princess about to walk down the aisle. A sleek ivory color dress hugs every curve of her body. I can't drag my gaze away from her as we make our way through the crowds and down toward the gardens.

Her face is sweetly serene.

"You came," I say in shock. I honestly didn't think she'd accept my invitation to return to Black Light. My eyes never leave her as she moves through the greenery of the darkened garden. The leaves have turned an almost black where we've strolled. There are crowds from the party, but the corner we've found is secluded.

"I didn't want to," she offers, but doesn't turn my way.

I watch her trail her delicate fingers over the leaves, touching them the way I want her to touch me. We haven't been together in two weeks. And with every passing minute, I ache, I feel a physical pain not being near her.

I was right when I told her I'd loved before. I did love Siobhan, but with Roisin, she is so much more to me. She's my breath, my heartbeat, and the life-force that runs through my veins.

"I wanted to walk away, Kian," she tells me. "But." Her words stall. She turns to meet my gaze dead-on. "Days without you are torture, weeks without you hurt, they make me bleed inside, and when I imagined spending my life without you… that is not something I want to fathom."

She steps toward me, closing the distance that she put there, then she gently places her palms on my chest. The heat of her touch almost has my restraint snapping violently, but I rein it in, just for a few more moments.

I want to take her inside. Into one of the private rooms where I can bind her to the bed and have my wicked way with her. She tilts her head, offering me a glimpse of her slender throat, and I can't stand it anymore. My mouth is on her flesh, suckling and licking, tasting the sweetness that is the woman I love.

Her hands fist my shirt, tugging me impossibly closer to her. It's as if she wants to climb inside me as much as I want to be inside her. "Take me to a room. I want to play." She whimpers when I bite her neck, sucking hard, leaving my mark on her body.

Lacing my fingers through hers, I tug her toward the mansion. Inside, we make our way through to Black Light following all security procedures as fast as we possibly can. Once we're in one of the private rooms, I release her hand and saunter toward the bed, seating myself on the edge. I look at her.

"You're in charge tonight, sweetheart," I inform her.

Her brows lift in shock as she regards me. A playful smirk curls her full red lips. I watch as she strolls toward me, her hips swaying hypnotically.

She nears me where I'm perched watching her and leans in so her supple mouth is at my ear and whispers the words that only make my cock ache painfully to thrust deep within her and bury myself inside her womb. "I'm no longer on the pill."

The floor-length silk dress she's wearing pools around her feet, and I'm met with the porcelain skin I love to mark. Her body is encased in lace and silk lingerie. A corset hugs her torso, the bright red ribbons binding it to her form. Her panties are lace, with crimson ribbons tied into bows on either hip.

"Fuck," I growl, my cock hardening at the sight.

She spins on her heel, affording me a view of her pert ass, and I note the panties are actually a thong. The thin string that disappears between her cheeks makes me want to rip them from her body.

"Sweetheart, you better do something or I'm going to fuck you like a bad girl. I'm going to ravage you until you're a whimpering, boneless mess."

She giggles, not responding, and I realize this is what she

wants. She's taunting the beast. Bending at the waist, she reaches back, spreading the cheeks of her beautiful ass, offering me a glimpse of the red jeweled plug before she rises to full height.

"Jesus," I bite out the word, gritting my teeth to stop myself from blowing my load like a teenage boy. Rising, I saunter toward her, grabbing both wrists. "You want to play?"

She nods.

I tug her toward the bed. Watching her climb on slowly makes me even harder than I was before. My cock is solid steel behind my zipper.

"Hands at the foot end of the bed," I tell her.

She moves at my instruction, silent and obedient. I grab the leather cuffs and return to where she's kneeling. I bind both wrists, then lock them in place on the hook that's bound to the sleek pole at the end of the bed.

"Ass up," I tell her, while I tug the ribbons on her underwear, causing the items to fall free of her body. Once she's naked, I grab one of the crops and watch as she waits.

Anticipation trickles through her. I see it when she trembles. Allowing the silence to envelop us both, I wait, watch, and smile when she moves her head to look where I am.

"Did I tell you to look at me?"

"No, Master," she whispers.

Raising my hand, I bring the crop down onto her ass. A small patch of red appears. I continue my assault. When the leather licks at her pussy, she cries out as her body shudders.

"More, Master, please," she begs and I grab a flicker whip, the small leather implement will be a welcome new toy to test on my pretty little pet, knowing it will offer her the pleasure she seeks. Her flesh marked with shades of red. When I lean in, planting a kiss on her back, I inhale her scent.

"You're wet, sweetheart," I tell her. "You're practically drenching the bed, wanton and needy," I continue, my voice heavy with desire.

"Please, Master," she whimpers. "I want you."

I don't offer a response. Instead, I toe off my dress shoes, along with my socks. Unbuttoning my shirt, I shrug it off. Next to follow are my slacks, and lastly, my boxers. Once I'm naked, I crawl onto the bed behind her, lifting her hips, lewdly opening her to my gaze.

"You have such a pretty cunt," I tell her, stroking her slick core with my fingers, wetting two digits in her juices. I don't penetrate her. Instead, I tease her, knowing what she needs, but not giving it to her.

The small plug in her ass glints under the lights in the ceiling, and I grip it with two fingers, twisting it inside her, tugging it slowly, then pushing it in once more. Fucking her with the plug, causing whimpers that send jolts of pleasure to my cock.

I fist my shaft, running the tip over her lips, coating myself in her arousal. Watching how she soaks me only makes me want more. With control of her butt plug, and my cock at her pussy, I smirk before driving into her balls deep.

The cry that's wrenched from her throat is otherworldly as I pump my cock inside her body, all the while twirling the plug inside her. I know she's full. Feeling both of her tight holes filled must be something else entirely.

"Oh God," she mewls, a sound I'll never tire of. My hips slam into her ass, watching the gentle ripple of her body, which only makes me smirk. Fuck, she's perfection. I swat her ass, my red handprint on the fleshy globe.

I pull out and thrust in, slow at first, taunting her, but the torture is far too much for me to handle. My body is hers as I still. "Fuck me, baby girl, show me how much you missed me."

She takes the lead, pushing herself back onto my cock, again and again. The sight is addictive. I can watch her ride me every day of my life and that's exactly what I intend to do. As soon as I feel her body flutter around my cock, I reach for the plug and tug it from her tight ass, causing her to cry out. She calls my name over and over as her body finds euphoria, the pulsing of her cunt milking my release deep within her womb, and the thought of her pregnant with my child only causes me to grip her hips in a viselike hold and bury myself deep, hoping to see her swollen soon enough.

EPILOGUE

Roisin

Stalking into the bedroom, I find Kian tangled in white sheets, his body still naked from our evening of debauchery. I love looking at him while he's silent, asleep. The peace that surrounds him is something I get used to in the early hours of the morning.

The sun isn't above the horizon yet. There's nothing more than a glimmer of gold and burnt orange peeking through the curtains. I love his home. Our home. I pad over to the nightstand, lifting the large, fancy camera, and bring it to my eye. I snap a shot of Kian while he's still sleeping.

"Are you being a creeper?" he mumbles into the pillows and I can't help smiling. He doesn't move, so I snap another, and another. My gaze eating him up, devouring him like only I can.

"I've learned from you, Mr. Creeper," I tease, knowing it will earn me a spanking, but I don't care. I love when he binds me to his bed, to anything really. How his hands inch over my skin, burning me like a fire has been lit deep within my core.

This time, he does roll over, causing the sheet to fall from his hips. The slight V muscles that point to his hard shaft are visible and I snap a quick shot before he grips my hips, pulling me over him. I straddle his waist, my core nestled over him, and I revel in the deep growl that rumbles in his chest.

"Lift your hands above your head," I tell him, not expecting him to obey, but he does. A smile tilts his lips sexily as he regards me from the pillows. The white sheets beneath him make his skin look more tanned than he already is. Those eyes, those piercing eyes look right through me as I take a photo of him again. His arms aren't big, but the muscles are defined in a way that makes me tremble.

Kian is strong. He's beautiful and rugged, but he's also caring and romantic. Even when he doesn't want to admit it. I'm staring at him through the camera, his face a picture of happiness and relaxation as his hand reaches beside him.

"Take a photo now," he orders as he brings his hand up to the lens, close enough for me to focus on the object he's holding. A single four-carat diamond, sapphire cut, set in white gold. The same ring that we saw two weeks ago when we went on vacation to New York.

I lower the camera, but he's become blurry as I blink away my tears. One falls, trickling down my cheek, but Kian's thumb swipes it away as quickly as it appeared.

"Is this what I think it is?" I rasp, emotion making it difficult to swallow.

"This is everything you think it is, sweetheart," he offers, scooting up until his back is against the plush velvet headboard, and I'm still perched on his lap. "I want this, I want you," he tells me, lifting my wrist. He holds my hand so gently, bringing it to his mouth as he plants a kiss on my knuckles. "Say yes."

"Is that an order, or do I have a choice?" I quip playfully, earning me a swat on my ass.

"Do you want a choice?" His dark brow lifts in question, his eyes sparkling with challenge.

I shake my head and whisper, "No."

"No? No, you don't want a choice or no, you don't want to spend the rest of your life with me?"

Giggling, I lean forward, kissing him deeply before I murmur across his full lips, "Yes, I want to marry you. No, I never had a choice. You stole my heart the moment you looked at me."

His mouth curls into a smile. He slips the ring onto my finger, then flips us easily so he's cocooned above me, his body resting between my thighs. "And you stole everything from me the moment you smiled, sweetheart," he murmurs across the sensitive spot at the curve of my neck. Soft kisses and gentle touches are not normally Kian's specialty, but he does them so well.

My mind is adrift with thoughts of a wedding. Me in a white dress, although something tells me I'd need to wear black after all the things I've done with Kian.

"Look at me," he orders, dragging me from the illicit thoughts in my mind. "I love you, beautiful princess." His words are my salve, they always will be.

"And I love you, dark knight," I tease, lifting my hips against his, causing his cock to jolt as it presses against my clit, taunting me. My panties are in the way, and I wish he'd tear them from me, but he doesn't.

A groan tumbles from him, and I continue teasing him. "You're a bad girl, Rosie," he tells me. Leaning in, he captures my earlobe in his mouth and suckles on the tingling flesh. His hips press me into the mattress, his cock rubbing against my aching center as he teases my neck with soft kisses and harsh bites.

"Please, Kian," I beg, arching my back, causing my breasts to press against his hard chest. But he doesn't give me what I need. He merely taunts me even more.

"Let's have breakfast, then I'll think about making my soon-to-be wife come." He chuckles, rising up and pulling me along with him.

"You're no fair." I can't help pouting as he drags me along to the kitchen. I settle on the chair and watch him move about the space. He's perfect in so many ways, and even though he needs the control, there are times he allows me to have it as well.

"I'm always fair, sweetheart, and that ring on your finger will ensure that you're forever mine to play fair with."

I nod in agreement, because when I glance down at it, my heart fills with excitement at spending my life with him. At giving him a family he so desperately wants and needs. And to grow old with him.

This is my forever.

He is my life.

And I wouldn't have it any other way.

Kian

I SIP MY COFFEE. WATCHING THEM IN THE GARDEN. I CAN'T BELIEVE I almost lost my little girl. Roisin and Cassidy are lying on their loungers under the biggest umbrella we could find. My two girls.

They're giggling about something I can't hear, but the happiness that floats toward me is enough to confirm they're growing more comfortable with each other each time Cassidy visits.

"Daddy!" A screech comes from my daughter, along with my wife.

I'm racing from the house in seconds to find them both being splashed by Harry, the Labrador Cassidy wanted for Christmas.

"Harry's being bad." My daughter pouts as he shakes the water from his fur. Sprinkles of droplets fly everywhere, soaking both girls.

Roisin is six months pregnant with our son as she scurries from the lounger and curls herself under the crook of my arm. Her body is utter perfection, swollen with my baby, but she still fits me like she's my missing piece.

"Let's go inside for a little while." I lace my fingers through both Cassidy's fingers as well as Rosie's.

We head indoors, and I flop on the sofa.

"Let's get this puzzle finished," Rosie suggests, and Cassidy is already on her chair, waiting at the table. They sit side by side, building a two-thousand-piece puzzle I bought them.

"Look at this one, Ros," my daughter whispers, showing her stepmother which piece fits where. Once again, it's only moments later that they're giggling.

I can't help smiling as I watch the scene.

I'm happy.

My life is complete.

And I wouldn't have it any other way.

The End

STOP! Don't go yet! We'd love it if you'd leave a review for the book you just finished. And keep reading for more information about the Black Light world and Dani Rene titles.

ABOUT THE AUTHOR

Dani is an international bestselling author and proud member of the Romance Writer's Organization of South Africa (ROSA) and the Romance Writers of America (RWA).

A fan of dark romance that grabs you by the throat and doesn't let go. It's from this passion that her writing has evolved from sweet and romantic, to dark and delicious. It's in this world she's found her calling, growing from strength to strength and hitting her stride.

On a daily basis, she has a few hundred characters, storylines, and ideas floating around in her head. From the feisty heroines she delivers to the dark, dominant alphas that grace the pages of her books, she promises light in a world filled with danger and darkness.

She has a healthy addiction to reading, TV series, music, tattoos, chocolate, and ice cream.

FIND DANI ONLINE

FB GROUP: DANI'S DARKLINGS

IG: @danireneauthor
FB Page: DaniReneAuthor
GR: Dani René
Amazon: Dani René
Newsletter: http://bit.ly/2sAy5dU
BookBub: Dani René
Twitter: @DaniReneAuthor

ALSO BY DANI RENÉ

Stand Alones

Ace of Harts

Love Beyond Words

CUFFED

Fragile Innocence (A dark ménage romance)

Perfectly Flawed

Taboo Novella's

Sunshine and the Stalker

His Temptation

Austin's Christmas Shortcake

Crime and Punishment (Newsletter Exclusive)

Sins of Seven Series

Kneel (Book #1)

Whisper (Book #2)

Indulge (Book #3)

Ruthless (Book #4)

Four Fathers Series

Kingston

Four Sons Series

Brock

Carina Press Novella's

Pierced Ink

Madd Ink

Broken Series

Broken by Desire

Shattered by Love

The Backstage Series

Between Love & Fire

Between Lust & Tears

Between Want & Fear

Forbidden Series

From the Ashes - A Prequel

Crave (Book #1)

Covet (Book #2)

BLACK COLLAR PRESS

Did you enjoy your visit to Black Light? Have you read the other books in the series?

Infamous Love, A Black Light Prequel by Livia Grant
Black Light: Rocked by Livia Grant
Black Light: Exposed by Jennifer Bene
Black Light: Valentine Roulette by Various Authors
Black Light: Suspended by Maggie Ryan
Black Light: Cuffed by Measha Stone
Black Light: Rescued by Livia Grant
Black Light: Roulette Redux by Various Authors
Complicated Love, A Black Light Novel by Livia Grant
Black Light: Suspicion by Measha Stone

Black Collar Press is a small publishing house started by authors Livia Grant and Jennifer Bene in late 2016. The purpose was simple - to create a place where the erotic, kinky, and exciting worlds they love to explore could thrive and be joined by other like-minded authors.

If this is something that interests you, please go to the Black Collar Press website and read through the FAQs. If your questions are not answered there, please contact us directly at: blackcollarpress@gmail.com.

WHERE TO FIND BLACK COLLAR PRESS:

- Website: http://www.blackcollarpress.com/
- Facebook: https://www.facebook.com/blackcollarpress/
- Twitter: https://twitter.com/BlackCollarPres

A SNEEK PEEK AT WHAT'S NEXT FOR BLACK LIGHT

Coming in November 2018

Black Light: Fearless **by Maren Smith**

Blurb:

Pregnant and alone, Kitty had no idea how far she'd have to flee the night she finally got up courage enough to run, but she never guessed she would end up halfway around the world or in the home, much less the arms, of dominant Australian whip-master, Noah Carver. The only question now is what did she fear more: returning to the abusive father of her child or staying with a man she was afraid to love?

Enjoy this Excerpt:

Hugging her towel, Kitty crept through the second kitchen archway, edging between the massive dining table and built-in china hutch, to peek out through the half-open drapes into the yard. She saw the radio first, sitting on the white-painted front porch rail, blaring its '80s music out into the yard where Noah was standing—no, not standing, dancing—step dancing, in form-fitting jeans, crocodile boots and worn tan hat, and a white t-shirt that fit him in a way that was at once loose and yet a second skin. She could see the ripple of muscle playing across his shoulders and back, bunching and flexing in his biceps as his arms moved to the beat, rising and falling, snapping out the rhythm with each of the whips he held, one in each hand. That was the source of the popping. Not one crack at a time, but two and three snaps to each fluid movement as he turned and stepped, and tapped his way through to the end of that Dire Straits song.

When it was over, the music paused long enough for him to reset himself. Head slightly bowed, he rolled his muscular shoulders, shook the whips out like long snakes in the dust around his feet, and then AC/DC started up. *Thunderstruck*. His foot started tapping. He found the beat, and then he began all over again. Fluid, graceful, line-dancing motions that he so effortlessly filled with a whole new accompaniment of tempo-keeping cracks from his whips.

She caught her breath, suddenly aware that her stomach was tightening and quivering right along with his punctuating music.

Abruptly retreating from the window, Kitty stood for a moment at the table, hands clutching and tightening and adjusting at her towel, feeling at once hot and flustered and confused and scared, and then stupid because she didn't know why. Two tiny steps forward could have carried her back to the window for a second peek, but she made herself turn away.

The heavenly aroma of coffee drifted from the kitchen.

She hugged herself, knowing she ought to get dressed, but also knowing there was no way she was going back into her bedroom. Not now, possibly not ever.

She wandered as far as the living room, stopping again between the dark yawning maw of the hallway leading back to spider-infested doom and the front door, with its multi-paneled glass windows that provided another peak at Noah, out in the yard.

A sparkle of gold drew her eye into the living room. There wasn't a lot of furniture to stumble around and useless decorations, but there were a lot of display boxes hanging on the walls. In each one, attached to a green-felt backcloth, was a coiled brown-plaited whip with a golden plaque the size of a business card. Noah's name was engraved on each one, with the division of whip cracking that he'd won—most of which read simply 'Mens' Champion'—and the year. There were fifteen of them total, and they spanned nine years' worth of achievements.

Scattered among them and along the fireplace mantel were pictures. Some of Noah at various ages; some of other people. Everybody had whips, and one was a newspaper clipping taken from the local paper in which the headline included both Noah's name and the 2000 Sydney Olympics, where apparently, he and others from the Australian Whipcrackers & Plaiters Association had put on the Opening Ceremony and, as the paper put it, opened the eyes of the world to the competitive sport of Australian whip cracking.

She was looking over his framed collection of Guinness World Record titles when the front door suddenly opened and Noah walked in. How she had missed hearing the music shut off, she didn't know. It wasn't as if he were trying to sneak up on her. The heavy tromp of his boots when he crossed the threshold, took one look at her in nothing but a towel, and abruptly stopped, was damn near deafening.

To his credit, he didn't ogle her. He kept his eyes locked with hers and any hint of discernible expression locked tight behind a mask she could not read. It was probably disapproval. It had to be disapproval, though there wasn't so much as a single censuring note in the way he finally said, "Rule Number Five, love. Admittedly, I did only specify shoes, but in my defense, I assumed you would know to put your clobbers on and not to go nuddy about."

Both whips were in his hand, coiled and tied. But every experience she had in regards to whips had taught her how easy it was to make them ready for use again. It would have been so easy, especially with that thought running wild in her head, to be afraid of him. And yet, with his face was void of expression and his tone careful not to be too scolding, he made no move to come at her.

He smelled like sunshine, too, her brain supplied.

Like that should make a difference, she wanted the rest of her to argue, but in some weird way… it did make a difference. It was all she could smell, the sunshine, the dust and leather of his boots, the faint spice of his deodorant or soap, and the warm coffee spreading through the house. It made such a difference that, standing here, staring at him with those whips in his hand, her nipples budded into tight little peaks and a single thump of warm neglect pulsed between her tensing legs. She clutched her towel, tightening her thighs in an effort to kill the sensation, but like ripples on a still pound, that thump spread up through her belly, becoming a series of smaller pulses that she could feel steadily throbbing out through her sex and into her womb.

Made in the USA
Middletown, DE
04 March 2020

85753479R30117